WATERFALL KISSES

KRISTA LAKES

ZIRCONIA PUBLISHING, INC.

ABOUT THIS BOOK

When Charlotte Page first met Leo Westbrook, she was a shy, skinny teenager on the verge of becoming a woman. The moment the naked, chiseled Adonis mistakenly walked into her room, she was lovestruck. Leo was perfect in her eyes, and he proved it by helping create a billion-dollar business with Charlotte's brother.

Even before he became a billionaire, Leo always had women throwing themselves at him. But the only woman he really wanted was the one he couldn't have. Because Charlotte was his best friend and business partner's little sister, he couldn't afford to let her get too close. Yet he found himself unable to resist her. With each passing day, her charms threatened to overcome his defenses.

After a decade of being his friend's blushing, stuttering little sister, the man of Charlotte's dreams finally noticed her. After one tropical kiss and a night of passion, her fantasy finally seemed to be coming true. However, when a lie from Leo's past caught up with him, it prompted her to question everything she thought she knew about the man she loves.

Leo always knew that being with Charlotte wasn't meant to be. Even if she could forgive him for his decade-long deception, he knew it would be better for her if he walked away. Yet sometimes, love is stronger than lies. Will Charlotte and Leo find a way to be together, or will they be left with nothing but memories of their waterfall kisses?

❧

I kicked off my shoes and stepped into the lagoon. The water was cold, but it felt good against the Caribbean heat. Leo was right beside me, holding my hand tightly in his.

I waded out, holding my dress up to keep it out of the water.

"Why don't you just take it off?" he asked, managing to keep a straight face.

I hesitated. I only had a pair of undies on underneath the dress. Thong undies.

Was I ready for that?

It took me all of two seconds to decide that yes, yes I was ready for that. I'd been ready to be naked with Leo for ten freaking years. But I didn't want to be the only one getting naked.

"Only if you do, too," I replied, slowly inching the skirt of the dress up. Leo's eyes went to my bare thigh, the blue slowly disappearing to the dilating black of his pupils.

"Done," he said, whipping his shirt over his head and tossing it to the shore.

I nearly dropped my dress hem. His chest gleamed in the sun, muscled and perfect. He liked to keep active, but he usually stayed dressed around the office, so I didn't get a regular look at his body.

He smirked as he caught me looking. "Were you going to

take it off or what?" he teased, loosening the zipper on his shorts. My breath caught a little. It was time. I closed my eyes and took a deep breath, hoping that I looked as good to him as he did to me.

I pulled the dress up and over my head, balling it up and tossing it onto the pebbly beach. I stared at the water for a moment before raising my eyes to look at Leo. Part of me was terrified that he'd back out, suddenly remembering that I was Bastian's little sister and he shouldn't be looking at me like that.

But he didn't. He stared and the reaction in his boxers told me that he didn't think of me as anyone's little sister. Without looking, he tossed his shorts behind him, narrowly missing dropping them in the water.

I hugged my arms around me as he came closer. I stood mid thigh deep in the water. He looked me up and down, desire and admiration filling his face. I bit my lip a little, still nervous as to what he was going to say next.

"Wow," he whispered, stopping in front of me. "Just wow."

"Thanks," I giggled, suddenly giddy and ridiculously happy. "You look pretty 'wow' yourself."

"You'd know," he teased. "The first time I met you, I was naked."

"I remember," I replied, my voice suddenly going husky. I took a step forward. "But you looked more like this-"

And then I pulled down his boxers, soaking them in the water...

∿

Author's Note: The beginning of this book dovetails with the end of <u>Sunrise Kisses</u>. You do not have to have read it to get this book, but it might increase your enjoyment. Hope you like it!

Don't forget to sign up for my newsletter! You'll be the first to see my new covers, comment on new books of mine, and always know when books are available for free or on sale!

1

——

"Do I know you?"

I looked up from the event table I was desperately trying to organize. A man wearing a salmon pink polo shirt with khaki shorts that were just a little too short stood in front of me. He reminded me of a plastic Ken doll with his bleached hair that was gelled into submission and what looked like a fashion shoot pose.

"Excuse me?" I asked. There was a massive gala tonight to showcase the items available for auction tomorrow, and this table needed to be set up and fixed. The auction of this multi-million dollar Caribbean estate was very important to me and really, *everything* needed to be perfect, but I was focusing on this table for the moment.

The man grinned. "Do I know you? Because I'm having a hard time recognizing you with your clothes on."

I stared at him, dumbfounded. There was no way he could be serious.

"That's seriously what you're going with?" I asked after a moment. I was way too busy for crappy pick up lines. "You're at a million dollar event hosted by a billionaire on a private island wearing knock off sunglasses and a fake tan, and that's the pick-up line you're going with?"

The guy took a step back, clearly not expecting that to be my answer. He must be used to girls who would giggle and blush. I was not a giggle and blush kind of girl. At least not today.

"Just trying to start a conversation with a pretty lady." He put on what I assumed must be his most charming smile. It didn't work on me in the slightest.

I pushed my glasses back up my nose and then pointed to the auction items clearly scattered on the table along with my tablet and paperwork. The gala was in just a few hours and I had more work than I knew what to do with. I definitely didn't have time to deal with Pick-Up-Artists. "Do I look like I want a conversation right now?"

"Um, well..." The man finally stopped staring at my chest and noticed that I was actually busy.

"I'm busy. Go away." I picked up my tablet, scrolling to the inventory list to double check that this table had all the appropriate items. My brain was already busy remembering where the event planner was setting up the dinner tents, that my boss still had two more appointments today, when the caterer was unpacking and prepping, if the auctioneers were prepared, and remembering to remind security to keep a handle on the journalists covering the event. I wanted journalists, not paparazzi.

The man cleared his throat, not so subtly asking for more attention than I was willing to give. I counted to five before looking up. "What?"

"I'm looking for someone, and you look like you work here," he said with another "charming" smile.

"Is that another pickup line? Because it's terrible." I glanced around the room. There were at least four other people who clearly looked like they worked here, but none of them were under the age of fifty or female. No wonder I was the center of his attention.

He had the audacity to roll his eyes at me. I did not have time for this right now.

"I'm looking for a C. Page. I'm supposed to report to him for the auction. I was hoping you might help me find him," the man replied, trying once again to ooze charm.

"Who are you?" I asked, doing my best to remain pleasant despite the fact my blood was starting to boil. I was C. Page, and most certainly not a "he."

"My name's Chad Malin," he replied, holding out his hand. I didn't take it since my own were full of work accessories. He withdrew after a moment, but still wore that sleazy smile. "I'm the head auctioneer at the auction tomorrow. I could get you tickets if you want."

Something about the name Chad stuck in my memory as someone to avoid, but I was too busy to expend the brain power trying to remember why at the moment.

"I don't need tickets. I'm C. Page, as in Charlotte Page, as in Mr. Sebastian Belrose's- the billionaire who is throwing this little shindig- Personal Assistant C. Page." I set the tablet down with a thunk. I thought about adding that Bastian was also my brother, but decided against it. Professional was what I needed. "I'm the one you were supposed to report to three hours ago in order to prep for the auction since you decided not to show up yesterday. You were left several messages."

"Aw, you're too pretty to be in charge," Chad drawled, smiling widely. For a moment, I wondered what the extradition laws for murder were from the Caribbean. Probably not worth it, but still tempting.

"And you are apparently too dumb to work here," I replied, letting my anger get the best of me for a moment. "I'll get another auctioneer."

"Wait," he said quickly, taking a step forward and panic crossing his features for a moment. "I'm sorry, miss. I'm just stressed about my fiancée. She's going through a really rough time in her life right now, her dad's got this heart thing, and-"

"-And that's why you thought it was a good idea to hit on me?" I finished for him. "Your fiancée?"

Chad's mouth opened and closed like a fish. I wanted to fire him. I really, really wanted to fire him and ban him from the mansion, but the auction was tomorrow and I didn't actually have the time to go find another auctioneer. Being on a Caribbean island, there just weren't a lot of professional auctioneers walking around and I was short on time just to get the necessary things done without adding something new to my plate. As much as I hated it, I couldn't really fire him.

"Mr. Malin, the auction is tomorrow and I expect you to be there and on time. Early even." I picked up my tablet and indicated to a room down the hall. "They are prepping the materials in the library, which is just down the hallway and to the left. You'll recognize it because of the books and the fact that there are two other auctioneers, including your boss, inside it. I would advise you to go there. *Now*."

"Yes, ma'am," he said quickly, turning to walk away. I strongly considered throwing the vase on the table at the back of his head. He shouldn't have riled me so much, but I was already behind and I still needed to get ready for the gala as well as check on a billion other little details. My head was starting to throb with the stress of it all.

"You look about ready to punch someone's lights out," a deep male voice said from my left side.

I smiled. That voice was from the one person who could make my bad day better just by saying hello. My stomach did the familiar flutter it always did whenever Leo was around. The one where love-sick butterflies danced an Irish jig that made me giddy. My headache went away.

"Hi, Leo," I said, turning and smiling. Just the sight of him made my day better. It didn't matter that I'd had an unrequited crush on him for the past ten years, his effect on me was still the same. I thought he was the most handsome man I'd ever met and the ten years since I'd met him had only increased that opinion.

He was certainly taller and had added muscle since he was eighteen, but the unruly dark hair and striking blue eyes still stole my heart. But really, it was his smile, the one he was giving me right now, that made me melt. When he grinned at me, I couldn't stop my heart from fluttering and my hormones to spiral out of control. That smile made me feel like the center of the world.

I cocked my chin in the direction of the annoying auctioneer. Instead of going to the library, he was trying his *"do I know you?"* line on one of the catering assistants prepping appetizer tables.

"What do you know about hiding a body?" I asked Leo, shooting death ray glares at Chad.

Leo laughed, turning his head to look and giving me a view of his profile. I could look at his strong jaw and straight nose for hours. My hand went to my hair and quickly let it out of the tight bun I had it up in. Dark waves spilled out over my shoulders, and I hoped that it looked pretty. It was irrational and I knew I sounded like a high-school girl trying to impress a boy, but I wanted to look my best for Leo.

Not that he'd notice, or care. I could be stretched out wearing nothing but a smile and he'd probably just walk on by. As far as he was concerned, I was practically his sister. It didn't help that my older brother was his best friend. As much attraction as I felt toward him, he made it very clear he wasn't interested in anything more than a friendship. I was just Bastian's kid sister to him, not a woman and certainly not anyone he'd do anything more than give a platonic kiss on the cheek.

"That guy?" he asked, jabbing his thumb toward the auctioneer. "Want me to go beat him up for you?"

I giggled. His simple joke had my heart beating way too fast and I knew a blush was searing across my cheeks. It wasn't fair that he had this reaction on me. I had hoped that my attraction to him would fade, but it never had. If anything, I just liked him more the longer I knew him. I was able to handle being a billionaire's assistant and staring down powerful men, but one look from Leo turned me into a flustered schoolgirl.

"Oh god, it's him," I whispered as the realization of who Chad Malin was hit me. I closed my eyes and shook my head. No wonder I hated him. "I just figured out who he is."

"Please tell me he's not your date for tonight." There was a protective edge to his voice that made my heart rise. But I knew it was just because he looked out for me like a brother. I wasn't Leo's type. Even though he seemed to favor brunettes, the last three women he'd dated gave rocks a run for their money on intelligence. He liked them pretty and dumb.

I could pretend I was pretty, but dumb wasn't in my vocab.

"No, not my date. He's Ava's ex. Her awful, horrible ex."

"Ava?" Leo thought for a moment, trying to place the name. "The pretty redhead from the other night? Who left right before you barfed all over me?"

The blush that had finally started to fade came back with a vengeance and my heart sank with embarrassment. I wanted to block that memory out of my mind for as long as possible. Me-- unable to hold my liquor and throwing up all over Leo- was not the way I wanted him to think of me.

Ava Fairchild was the auction appraiser, and while she was out here appraising the mansion for auction, the two of us had become friends. I had taken her out for a girl's night at a local bar when Leo showed up.

Ava, being a true friend, had left me alone with Leo. It should have been a dream come true. It should have been fantastic and wonderful, and a chance to flirt and impress Leo in a non-work environment without Bastian there to interrupt. It was basically a date.

Except I was nervous had gulped a very strong drink on an empty stomach.

And then puked all over him.

"I'm still really sorry about that," I whimpered, hiding my face in my hands. Of all the people to get sick on, I had gotten sick on the man of my dreams.

"You've already sent me three shirts to replace the one." Leo laughed, putting his hand on my shoulder. I thrilled at his touch, but didn't uncover my face. "It's fine. You just aren't allowed any alcoholic drinks around me until you learn how to hold your liquor."

I uncovered my eyes. He was smiling at me with warm blue eyes. I grinned weakly. Someday, I was sure I would find the whole story humorous.

"Anyway, I remember her," Leo continued. "She was very sweet. That's her ex?"

I glared at the man in the salmon shirt. "Yeah. Guy's a real loser. Ava walked in on him cheating and ended everything months ago, but he's telling anyone with two X chromosomes that 'his fiancée' is just going through a rough patch."

"Wow. He looks really broken up about it," Leo observed as Chad brushed the catering girl's hair out of her face. Unfortunately, she looked like she was falling for his act. The guy was attractive enough, but his tactic was way too obvious. All he wanted was in her pants.

"Now I really want to punch his lights out," I said, feeling protective. "If he tells Bastian that he's back with Ava... I might kill him." I looked up at Leo and grinned hopefully. "You'd help me with the body, right?"

"Always," he replied without hesitation. Warm, fuzzy feeling drifted through my middle. He frowned slightly. "Why would you care what he tells Bastian about a fake fiancée anyway? People are always making up bullshit reasons to talk to us. It's part of being a billionaire."

I looked up at him, surprised. I thought he knew about Ava and Bastian, but apparently not. "Have you talked to Bastian in the past couple of days?"

"Not really," he said with a shrug. "I've been busy finishing up that giant phone app thing that our company is working on. You know, the one that we've been working on non-stop for the past month?"

I rolled my eyes at him. Considering the two of us just spent a week working eighteen-hour days to make the app a reality, there was no way I could forget. "So you haven't noticed the change in him?"

Leo shrugged. "He seemed moodier than usual, but it's

Bastian. He's tall, dark and brooding. That's why we all love him."

"He's in love with her," I informed Leo.

"The caterer?" he asked.

"No! Ava!" I smacked his arm and he grinned at me. "Bastian is in love with Ava."

"Oh, good for him." Leo looked at me like I was slightly crazy. "Why would this guy matter then? He's a nobody. Why believe him?"

"The problem is that Ava isn't here," I explained. "Apparently, they had a fight and she left. She's at home being an idiot until she realizes that she loves him and comes back."

"You sound like a romance novel, you know that, right?"

I smacked his arm again, this time harder. He laughed.

"Shut up, I'm serious," I said. "The two of them are head-over-heels crazy in love, but they're both being too dumb to do anything about it. I'm about ready to send someone to kidnap Ava and bring her here. It's either that, or acciden-tally have the private helicopter land on her lawn the next time Bastian gets on it."

"So Bastian's in love, huh?" Leo watched the auctioneer flirt with the caterer for a moment. "That does explain why he cussed me out for stealing his pen this morning. He did seem a little crankier than usual."

"If Bastian hears Mr. Stupid Hair's fiancée nonsense..." I shook my head. "It would kill Bastian if he thought Ava was with someone else."

"Mr. Stupid Hair?" Leo repeated, raising his eyebrows.

"He's making me mad and I can't think straight when I'm mad," I informed him. Instead of smacking his arm again, I tried to push him out of the way as I moved around the table. Except he was rock solid under my palms and didn't even budge. What would those muscles look like naked... under my fingers...

Stop it. He's not yours. I told myself.

"You sure are cute when you're mad," Leo informed me. I knew he was trying to tease me, but I couldn't help but flush with pleasure at being called cute. Damn him and how he always managed to tie me up in knots. Even when I was irritated with him, even though he would never feel the same way about me, I couldn't help but be charmed by him.

A sharp slap rang out through the main entrance and we both turned to see the caterer storming off while Chad held a hand to his cheek.

"Well, my day just got a little better," I said.

Leo chuckled. "I'm here to make it even better."

The warm gooey feeling filled my heart again. He didn't know it, but he had already made my day better just by smiling at me. He always did. "And how are you going to do that?"

"Check your email," he said with a smug smile.

I narrowed my eyes suspiciously, but pulled up my email on my tablet. The newest one was from Toby, Leo's personal assistant informing me that the guest list was finalized and the parking situation I had been struggling with was taken care of.

"What is this?" I scrolled through the email, seeing more things on my to-do list crossed off by Toby. "How?"

"Toby wanted to help you out," Leo informed me with a warm smile. "He knows you've been busy with the auction as well as the app stuff, and yet you still had the time to help him out last week. He actually insisted he help."

"What?" I looked up in surprise. "Toby hates me. He did all this?" I asked, glancing through the work. He had done a great job and was completely saving me.

Leo had hired Toby to be his personal assistant a little over a year ago, despite my objections. He had a decent resume, but there were so many more qualified candidates. I never understood why Leo was adamant that his long-lost college buddy get the job when I had perfect assistants with all the training needed lined up. Something about Toby rubbed me the wrong way, but Leo had insisted.

Apparently, the extra time I had to spend training Toby was finally paying off. Maybe, someday, we'd even get along.

"Does it help?" Leo asked, raising his eyebrows.

"This is fantastic," I said, closing the email and feeling a weight lift from my shoulders. "Thank you, Leo. This helps so much."

Leo held up his hands, deflecting my gratitude. "Don't thank me- thank Toby. It was all him."

"Still..." I didn't want to thank Toby. I wanted to thank Leo. I had a sneaky suspicion that it was Leo that had suggested it. It would be like Leo to do something wonderful and give the credit elsewhere. He was always doing stuff like that.

I thought about hugging Leo. I could hug him and it wouldn't be all that weird. We were friends after all. But I had the world's biggest crush on him and I was fairly sure that if I hugged him, I might burst into flames of desire.

So I just kept my distance and said a polite, "Thank you."

"So," Leo said, clearing his throat. His blue eyes focused on me and I suddenly felt like a high school girl meeting a rock star. He did it to me every time. Despite years to get over him, he still rendered me back into a love-struck teen with just a glance. "I'll see you at the gala tonight?"

I held up my tablet. "Since Toby got me caught up, yes." I grinned at him. "I have a dress and everything."

Leo's face lit up in a smile. "Excellent. Be sure to save me a dance. I know how Bastian likes to steal you for the whole night."

"He does not," I replied, trying not to roll my eyes. "He just likes to make sure I have a good time."

Leo took a step forward, and I was suddenly very aware of how close he was and how much I still wanted to hug him. To touch him. "Still, I want my dance tonight."

"It's yours," I whispered, breathless. Leo grinned and stepped back toward the main doors. Behind him, two men were moving one of the large cabinets to the auction area and through the open door I could see a taxicab dropping someone off. I frowned. I wasn't expecting anyone tonight to come in a taxicab.

A young woman with beautiful, dark red hair stepped out of the cab. It was my friend, Ava. She stood there, staring up at the big house and looking like a deer caught in the headlights. Her eyes were wide and rimmed with red, whether from crying or lack of sleep, I wasn't sure. Probably both.

Leo put his hand on my shoulder as he moved to look over my shoulder to see what had caught my attention. The simple touch set my body on fire in a way that I should have been used to by now.

"Looks like your friend is here," Leo said, removing his hand. I could still feel the weight of it on my shoulder and I missed it. I wanted so much more.

"This is going to make Bastian's night." I turned and grinned at him, thinking now of my friend and my brother. I knew Bastian was locked up in his room, moping over the fact that Ava left. The idea of presenting her, beautiful and looking like a princess, was too good to pass up. It would be the perfect fairy-tale ending. "Don't tell him, though. This is going to be the best surprise ever."

"Not a word." Leo mimicked zipping his lips and locking them shut. "You should go rescue her. She looks like she's about to bolt."

I grinned, handed him my tablet, and ran out the door to greet her.

2

___

"YOU CAME BACK!" I yelled, running down the steps toward Ava. My hair spread out behind me in the tropical heat. I jumped the last step, being careful of my heels before taking off at a run. Bastian never understood how I could do it, but I'd been wearing heels for work long enough to know how to run in them.

I wrapped her up in a giant hug. The last time I had seen her was a little over a week ago. We had become friends just before I had left to go work on the phone app for our company. That was right around the time she and Bastian realized they were perfect for each other and were giving the most obvious love-filled glances in the kitchen. I had been glad to get out of the house and give them some alone time.

To be honest, I was surprised when I came back to work on the auction and found out that she had gone back home, leaving my brother broken-hearted. Bastian claimed she said she just didn't fit his world, but that made no sense to me. They were so perfect together that I was having difficulty understanding why she had left, but somehow I knew she'd come back.

I was so glad to see her. Since she had been gone, Bastian had been mopey and miserable. I had missed her, and not just because of Bastian's mood swings. She was my friend, too.

"I'm glad to see you, too," she replied with a laugh.

I grinned at her, finally releasing her from my hug. "Bastian's going to flip. He's been absolutely no fun since you left."

"Where is Bastian?" Ava asked, her eyes going to the house and looking for him. "I need to talk to him."

"I'm sure you do," I said with a wink. They needed to do much more than talk. "But he's not here right now."

"Oh. Of course. I should have checked before I came..." Ava looked down at the ground, heartbreak filling her voice.

"But he'll be back for the gala tonight," I quickly promised. Poor Ava just looked more confused and all I wanted to do was hug her again. Apparently, being apart from Bastian had been as hard on her as it had been on him.

"Oh, he'll be back?" Relief flooded Ava's voice and her shoulders relaxed slightly. She looked exhausted. Her blouse was wrinkled and her shorts stained with the signs of fast food and travel. Her usually shiny, thick red hair was pulled back and brushed, but her eyes were red and her skin drawn and pale. If I looked up "travel-weary" in the dictionary, her picture would be there. Given that the island wasn't an easy place to get to without a private jet, I could only imagine the night she'd had.

"You are coming to the gala tonight, right?" I asked, already working on a plan. This was going to be my opportunity to play fairy godmother.

"Gala?" Ava sounded utterly confused. She frowned and

reached into her pocket, pulling out the golden ticket for the gala and auction. The paper was creased only once, as if she had stuck it in her pocket and forgotten about it. She now stared at it as if she were reading it for the first time. "I totally missed there was a gala on there."

I looked at her very small travel suitcase. There was no way an elegant evening gown was in there. "What are you planning on wearing?" I asked, knowing that she most likely didn't have a plan. If anything that made me love her more. Ava had just hopped on a plane with nothing in a rush to get to the man she loved. It was incredibly romantic.

I was a sucker for romantic.

"Um..." Ava blushed and looked down at her suitcase.

"Oh, good! You didn't bring anything. That makes this so much easier," I answered for her. My brain was already going at a million miles an hour on just how I was going to make this a night to remember. "It's always better to work with a blank canvas anyway."

"What?" Ava squeaked. She looked a little panicked and shell-shocked. I couldn't blame her. This must not have been at all what she was expecting.

"I've got just the designer for you," I said, thinking of the three brand new designer gowns hanging in my closet. They had been given to me by upcoming new artists specifically for this event and now I would be able to use at least two of them. I wrapped my arm around her shoulder and started to guide her up to the house. "This is going to be so much fun!"

Ava shot me a nervous look, but let me lead her forward. I wasn't the princess of the story, but I was going to be the fairy godmother and make sure that Ava and Bastian got their fairy tale ending.

"I'm going to make you the belle of the ball."

"Yes, yes, yes!" I exclaimed, finishing zipping up the back of the gown. It was perfect for Ava. The first time I saw the dress, I knew it would be too long for me, but since Ava was taller, it would fit her without even needing hemmed. It was as if it was made for her.

The dress was made of soft gold that flowed over her hips and made the woman in front of me appear lush and slender at the time. A gold lace overlay started right at her hips and continued down the length of the gown to create a train that was both romantic and stunning.

I hooked the top latch, making sure everything was in place. "I thought of you as soon as I saw this dress. It's perfect."

"It's not too much?" Ava asked, looking down at the rich lace fabric bodice.

I stood behind her and put my hands on her shoulders. With a gentle push, I moved her in front of the full-length mirror. "You look amazing. Stunning."

She smiled, taking in the dress for the first time. "I'm just nervous." Her smile faltered. "What am I going to say to him?"

"Tell him you love him," I told her without hesitation, squeezing her shoulders.

Ava looked up, the mirror reflecting the shock in her bright green eyes. "How did you know? I haven't said anything about how I feel..."

"Seriously?" I laughed, thinking of how obvious the feelings those two had were. "You just flew how many god-awful hours to come here? Besides, I knew you were in love with him from the moment I saw you two making flirty eyes over sandwiches. It wasn't exactly hard to figure out how you feel about him."

Ava giggled and blushed slightly. "Fair enough."

"He's going to be so happy to see you," I told her. I loved the way my brother had lit up while she was here. He was a different person- a happier person. He smiled more and the lines around his eyes disappeared when Ava was near. I could only imagine how happy the two of them would be together, if they would just give one another the chance.

Her smile faded with nerves. "Okay, no more talking about Bastian and how much of an idiot I am for not realizing I love him four days ago." She strengthened her smile. "New, but slightly related topic: Leo."

I froze, thinking of his hand on my shoulder this morning. Of his promised dance to me this evening. And how it was all a moot point. He'd never choose me.

"There's nothing on that front," I said with a sigh.

"Oh, come on- you two were alone all last week." Ava turned to look at me. Her skirt made a pleasant swishing sound with the movement. "Something must have happened?"

"First of all, we weren't alone. Gabe, the other owner of the company, was there. Second, we've been alone plenty of times and nothing's ever happened." I sighed. "And nothing ever will. He sees me as Bastian's little sister and nothing else. Nothing's going to change that. Believe me. I've tried."

Ava put her hands on her hips. The dress gave her an amazing hourglass shape. "What have you tried?"

"More of what *haven't* I tried?" I moved behind her and unhooked the the top of the zipper and began pulling it down. This fitting was just to make sure the dress fit and if we needed an emergency seamstress. She needed to be out of the dress for the hair and makeup ladies to work their magic. "I've tried being coy, setting up a romantic dinner, snuggling up to him, hell, I've even tried flat out asking him to kiss me, and nothing."

"You asked him to kiss you? And he said no?" Ava stepped out of the dress and put on a button-up shirt and shorts as I put the golden dress back on the hanger.

"Charlotte, you're drunk and don't know what you're saying," I said in a deep voice, trying to sound like Leo. "I don't want to do anything that could jeopardize my friendship with Bastian or you."

"Ouch." Ava winced.

"I've know him since I was thirteen. I've done my best to make it obvious how I feel about him, but he's not interested. He has made that super clear. For whatever reason, he doesn't want me and I don't see that changing any time soon." I shrugged. The ache in my heart was all too familiar. "I should be glad that he is my friend. I really need to learn how to be content with that."

"I'm sorry, Charlotte. When I saw the two of you together at that restaurant..." Ava shrugged and took the dress from me. "You two just seemed so perfect together."

"Thanks. I need to move on, I just..." I sighed, my heart aching. "I just can't."

Ava wrapped her arms around me, squishing me with the dress in the process. "At least we can be idiots about men together."

"I never said *I* was an idiot," I teased, hugging her back. "But you're right."

She grinned at me as a knock came on the door followed by the words, "Makeup lady."

"Go get pretty, Princess Ava," I said, releasing my friend from my hug. "I'll get my hair done and then we'll switch. It's a good thing I overbooked."

Ava went to the door and paused before opening it, turning to look back at me. "Charlotte?"

"Yes?"

"Thank you." Ava's gratitude and friendship flowed through her gaze and made me feel warm and loved.

"You're welcome." And I truly meant it.

As she walked away, I couldn't help but think about what I had just said. *"I never said I was an idiot."* But I knew that I was. I had been from the day that he walked into my life... completely naked.

3

———

10 Years Earlier...

I SAT CAREFULLY on the old wooden chair in Bastian's dorm room, looking around the room in awe.

So, this is what college looks like, I thought to myself. I had imagined it to look a little less like a boy's gym bag and more like an academic library, but I wasn't going to complain.

How many thirteen-year-olds got to go to college anyway? Or at least, got to visit their older brother in college and play pretend for the weekend.

I checked my watch. I still had another fifteen minutes before Bastian would come back from his "project." I rolled my eyes. *Project-* yeah right. It was obvious he was doing some cool college-y thing that he didn't want his little sister participating in. He just told me he had a group assignment he had to work on. *Sure, Bastian. Sure.*

The room was a small square with two twin beds on opposite sides, two desks and a small TV perched on a mini-fridge in the center. Per Bastian's instructions, I had the door open and the resident assistant had already checked on me twice.

Bastian's roommate and childhood best friend, Gabe, was going home for the weekend so I was going to use his bed. Gabe promised me that he would put clean sheets on the bed, but I had still brought my own.

I giggled at the thought of Gabe coming back to see the bright pink floral sheets now adorning his bed. He'd hate it. And deserve it. I'd known Gabe since he and his little sister, Chloe, moved in next door to my foster parent's house.

Chloe and I were best friends. Where Gabe and Bastian were always outside throwing footballs at each other, Chloe and I were busy getting ready to take over the world. I looked over at the girl-ified bed and decided I should take a picture to show Chloe. She'd love it.

I dug around in my backpack until I found the digital camera Bastian got me for my birthday last year and snapped a couple of pictures. After my weekend here on campus with Bastian, I would go home and share them with Chloe and we'd plan and dream what college would be like for us.

I hoped my real college experience would be more than just sitting around in a dorm room. I sighed. College was more boring than I had imagined.

And then *he* ran into the room.

Now, I liked boys. I no longer thought they had cooties and I had even kissed one. But the man standing in front of me blew that kid out of the water.

Plus, he was naked.

"Who are you?" the man sputtered, trying his best to hide himself behind his hands as he realized there was a thirteen-year-old girl in front of him. It was too late, I had already seen everything. "This is Bastian's room!"

I stared at him for a moment, not sure what was going on. This was more like what I thought college was going to be about, but now that it was happening, I didn't know what to do.

"Uh, I'm Bastian's sister," I informed him, throwing him Bastian's pillow, and shielding my eyes. "Who are you?"

The man's cheeks were a deep crimson as he pressed the pillow to his groin and stared at me for a second. He seemed to be evaluating his options. He sighed, shrugged, and clutching the pillow with one hand, reached out the other in greeting.

"I'm Leo," he said, sounding for all the world like this was an ordinary meeting and that he wasn't standing there butt naked with a pillow on his junk. "I live across the hall, and I'm locked out of my room."

"It's nice to meet you." I was impressed that this was how he was going to handle this. Personally, I'd be hiding in the closet, dying of shame, but he was owning it. I tentatively shook his hand, trying to ignore the very strange sensations it gave me. It was as if a fire was starting in the pit of my stomach and it made me feel all woozy and giggly. "You know Bastian, then?"

"Yup. We have English 101 together." Leo took his hand back and put it back on the pillow, looking cool as a cucumber. Bastian was going to be pissed when he found out where his pillow had been.

"Oh." I didn't know what else to say. What was I supposed to say to a naked man standing in my brother's room?

Leo glanced around the room, looking everywhere but at me. He was obviously incredibly embarrassed, but was trying desperately to stay polite and calm. "Would you mind seeing if your brother has a shirt and maybe a pair of shorts I could borrow? You know, until I can get back in my room?"

I looked down at the pillow without thinking and felt the blood rush to my face. I shouldn't look there. "Sure," I said quickly, standing up and trying not to look at him, even though I wanted to.

I went to Bastian's closet and thankfully found a t-shirt and gym shorts without having to dig through any drawers or laundry. For what was probably the first time in my life, I was glad Bastian was a little bit of a neat freak. The last thing I wanted was to come across his porn stash. That would have just been the cherry on an embarrassment sundae.

"Thanks," Leo said as I handed him the clothing. He waited for a moment, holding the clothes in one hand and the pillow in the other before raising his eyebrows. "You mind turning around?"

My blush went straight down to my toes. "Sorry!" I spun around quickly, pressing my hands to my flaming cheeks and wishing I could be just a little bit more suave.

"Okay, all done. You can turn around now," he said a much more relaxed voice.

I slowly turned. Leo was about the same height as my brother, so the clothes fit decently well. Even though I wasn't distracted by his naked muscles anymore, I was still trying not to stare. He was possibly the most handsome man I'd even seen.

His brown hair was messy and spiked up as if he had been running his hands through it. His shoulders were broad and his body was smoking. He had an easy-going smile now, but it was his eyes that captured me. They were blue, blue like the sky after a summer rain and full of a kindness and humor that I'd never seen anywhere else.

He was perfect.

I knew then that I was in love with him. Not for the fact that he had six-pack abs and an impressive package (or what I assumed was one, since I hadn't seen any before), but for those eyes. There was so much kindness and humor in them that I instantly loved him. I couldn't help it.

"Thanks for the clothes. I should go to the front desk and go get my keys so I can give these back to Bastian as soon as possible." He held out the pillow out to me. I nearly dropped it I was so awestruck. He grinned at me. "I don't think I caught your name."

"Charlotte," I whispered, my voice cracking and coming out with a squeak. I blushed harder. "My name's Charlotte."

"It's nice to meet you, Charlotte." He smiled wider and somehow got even more gorgeous. "I've always liked that name."

I giggled, suddenly nervous. Here was a handsome, college guy telling me he liked my name. I wanted him to like me so much it was hard to think of anything else. I was pretty sure Chloe would never believe me. "Thanks."

"I'll see you around, Charlotte," Leo said with a smile, heading toward the door. He paused, turning to look back at me. "Don't tell your brother I used his pillow. At least not until tomorrow."

He winked and I nearly melted into a puddle.

Handsome *and* funny.

I watched as he sauntered confidently down the hall.

College was awesome.

4

I stood in front of the mirror, holding my dress up to see how the ensemble would come together. My dark hair was curled and pulled back in a half-up style that was soft and feminine. I loved my makeup- not too much, but enough that my brown eyes looked big and my lashes could start a small windstorm. I felt pretty, and with my hair and makeup done, I just needed to get dressed, but I wanted a sneak peek of the final product.

"Not too shabby, Char," I said quietly. "Not too shabby."

Even on the hanger, the dress was beautiful. It was an off-the shoulder gown of royal blue and cut to hug the top half of my body before ending in a subtle mermaid tail at the bottom. The color was my favorite part, as well as the secret pocket where I could keep my phone without having to carry a purse all evening.

Ava's dress was perfect for her and this one was perfect for me.

I stared at the woman looking back at me for a moment. Sure, she had the same dark hair and dark eyes, short stature and same curves, but she didn't look like me. I'd done a thousand fancy galas, yet every time I looked in the mirror, I still saw the scrawny, terrified little girl with a runny nose.

Who would have thought that little girl would grow up to work with billionaires? I thought. *Let alone own enough company stock to be set for life herself. It was a long way from the past she had left behind.*

I was stronger now.

I smiled at the mirror, imagining tonight. The blue glinted in the light and shimmered, bringing out the highlights in my hair. I would look stunning in this dress. Maybe even stunning enough for Leo to finally notice and give me a chance.

Leo would take me in his arms, guiding me around the dance floor as if we were the only two people there.

"Why, Charlotte, you are the most beautiful woman I've ever seen," Leo would say, his eyes darkening with desire. *"I can't keep my feelings for you hidden any longer. I must have you."*

"Finally, Leo," I would whisper, breathless and happy.

He'd tuck his hand behind my neck, dipping me as the song ends and then leaning down, bringing his lips closer to mine until they finally...

A knock on the door shook me from my daydream.

"Can I come in?" Bastian's voice came through the door. Leave it to my older brother to ruin my fantasies about boys.

"Come on in," I called out, hanging the dress back up on a hook on the wall.

The door pushed open and my brother stepped into the room. He was already wearing his tux for the evening and looking handsome. I smiled. We weren't actually brother and sister, but as far as I was concerned we were.

Bastian and I were both foster children. When I came into the system, Bastian was the one who took care of me. My foster family had done their best to make us both feel welcome and loved, but it was Bastian who was my real family. We may not have shared genetic material, but I couldn't think of Bastian as anything but related to me.

"Can you fix my tie? I can't get the damned thing to do what it's supposed to do," Bastian growled, holding out the tie in frustration.

I chuckled. I knew he could tie his own tie, but it was now a ritual. Whenever Bastian had a formal event, he would have me tie his tie. I wrapped the silk tie around the back of his neck and went about knotting it.

"Do you have a jacket or something you can wear with that?" Bastian asked, his voice low and dangerous.

I looked up and followed his gaze to the dress hanging on the wall. "We're in the Caribbean, Bastian. I don't need a jacket."

"There's no way you're going out in that," he said gruffly, frowning as I slid the tie over and under itself. He put his hands on my shoulders, looking down sternly at me. "It's too revealing. No."

I rolled my shoulders, trying to loosen his grip. He didn't relax and his blue-gray eyes were serious. I knew he meant well, but I wasn't a little girl needing his protection any more either. Besides, this wasn't prom or a date. It was a billionaire's gala and the dress was perfectly acceptable. He was just projecting his heartbreak over his fight with Ava onto everything else.

"Sorry, Grump-face. This is my dress. Deal with it." I finished knotting and pulled the tie up tight, choking him a little. The gold threads in his tie would complement Ava's dress nicely.

Bastian glared at me, pulling down on the tie knot so he

could breathe. His shoulders were tensing and I could already hear the big-brother lecture coming. "Charlotte-"

"I don't want to hear it, Bastian," I warned as he opened his mouth. "As much as you'd like to, you do not control everything. I'm a big girl and this is my dress. And put a smile on your face. You have investors here tonight."

Bastian's frown deepened, darkening the scar that ran along the top of his eyes. I knew there were other, deeper scars, but that one was almost as good as a mood ring with him. Right now, it was telling me that he was far too wrapped up in his emotions.

"I do not try to control everything," he replied sullenly after a moment.

"Just keep telling yourself that," I told him. I stepped back and nodded at my work on his tie. He looked ready for Ava. "Now, unless you want to help me with my dress, you should get downstairs. The guests should be arriving and you're the main event."

Bastian sighed and turned for the door. His hand paused on the doorknob. "Have you heard from Ava?"

There was a quiet desperation in his voice that almost made me tell him she was here. But, that would ruin the surprise, so instead I simply asked, "What do you think?"

"Of course not." Bastian's shoulders slumped slightly. "She has someone else now.

"Bastian?" I asked, taking a step toward him. "Ava doesn't have someone else."

He looked back at me, his gray eyes clear yet broken. His face was calm, but there was a soft heartbreak in his voice. "It's not important."

"Bastian, she doesn't have someone else," I repeated. I was about to tell him that she was here, that she had come for him, but then he put on his business smile, the one he only wore for meetings that betrayed none of his true feelings.

"You sure you can't at least wear a scarf or something?"

"No, Bastian," I replied, shaking my head. He smiled, a hint of his usual humor shining through. I grinned back at him. He'd be with Ava in just a little bit. "I need to get dressed now."

He opened the door and closed it firmly behind him.

"Good lord, that man needs to get laid," I said under my breath. I thought about Bastian's "someone else" comment and shook my head. If that auctioneer had said anything, there were some hungry sharks that would get a free meal tonight.

5

———

After putting on my dress and shoes, I glanced in the mirror one last time and smiled at my reflection. This was definitely one of my favorite dresses so far and, as silly as it was, I hoped Leo thought so too. It irritated me how much his opinion mattered to me, especially considering that we weren't anywhere near being a couple. Someday, I would stop caring. Someday, I would find someone else to love and I would finally put these feelings for Leo aside. Someday, I would be smart and let him go. Just not today.

As it was, I suspected he would just tell me to put on a jacket, too.

With a shrug, I tossed my hair over my shoulder and went into the adjoining room to find Ava. She was standing in front of the mirror, mesmerized by her appearance.

"Holy crap. I do good work," I said, taking her in. Stunning didn't even come close to describing her. The dress was even better with her dark hair freshly curled and pulled back with a golden comb.

"You look gorgeous, Charlotte," Ava replied, her eyes barely leaving the mirror to look at me.

"What? This old thing?" I teased, walking around to take a better look at her. "Sebastian's going to lose his mind when he sees you."

"You're sure he'll be happy to see me?" she asked, pressing her knuckles into the lace at her stomach. Her cheeks were flushed but the rest of her was pale. I hoped she wasn't going to throw up from nerves.

"He's been the moodiest, most grumpy man I've ever had the misfortune of being around since you left. He hasn't even gone out paddle-boarding in the mornings. Just keeps talking about the dark." I shook my head, not really understanding the man I called brother. Heartbreak was not an emotion Sebastian dealt well with.

"I'm just nervous. I don't want to screw this up again." Ava's voice was barely above a whisper as she stared at the princess in the mirror.

I took her hands in mine. "He has been a mess without you. A broody, heartbroken, lovesick mess. He's going to be overjoyed to see you. I promise."

Ava stilled. "You know Bastian and I had a fight, right?" Her hands shook slightly in mine.

I reached up and fixed a stray strand of hair, pulling it from her eyes and tucking it back where it belonged. "Yes. I know."

"I said some terrible things..."

"He loves you," I assured her, taking her hands in mine again. "I know Sebastian. And I've never seen him the way he was with you. He was happy. And this past week..." I shook my head, remembering just how moody and grumpy he'd been without Ava around. The entire staff was on tiptoes and I was fairly certain his secretary was about to have a nervous breakdown. "This past week has been a nightmare without you."

"How could I have been so stupid?" Ava asked, her voice breaking and eyes starting to water. I hadn't meant to upset her, but apparently I had. I needed to work on my fairy god-mother skills.

"Don't you dare cry," I warned, knowing that in ten minutes the two of them would be happy lovebirds again. "It may be waterproof mascara, but I will not have you messing up all the work we just did."

"Sorry," Ava apologized. She sniffed and looked up at the ceiling, blinking rapidly and waving at her eyes in an attempt to make the tears go away.

"Sebastian Belrose loves you. I think he was smitten from the moment he saw you." I smiled, remembering the way he lit up around her and how he softened whenever he said her name. I'd never seen him do that for anyone else. If that wasn't love, then I was a crazy person.

"I don't think it was that fast. That first moment, I was kind of a jerk," Ava said, trying to joke about how she had basically told him off.

I laughed. The fact that she stood up to him was prob-ably part of the attraction. Anyone who could stand up to Bastian and not give into his brooding dark eyes and charming words was rare. "This is going to work out. I promise you. Just come downstairs." I smiled and checked the delicate silver watch on my wrist. "You ready?"

I didn't even wait for her answer before pushing her out the door. It was time for magic.

The hallway was quiet as we made our way to the top of the double staircase. The closer we came, the louder the murmur of voices and music became. Ava slowed and then tried to step back, but I wouldn't let her.

She balked harder and I followed her gaze to a man in a tacky knock-off suit. Chad the Auctioneer. I really needed to put feeding him to sharks on my to-do list. Or at least talk to Eli, Bastian's head of security, about having an "accident" occur. Given Eli's impressive military history, I had a feeling he could pull off something appropriately dark.

"No running," I whispered, pointing her toward Bastian instead of her evil ex. "Bastian's right there."

Ava shook like a leaf, but as soon as she saw him, I knew she wasn't going to back down. Strength went into her spine. I gave her a gentle push, more to get her moving than anything. The two of them deserved one another and I wasn't about to let them miss a moment.

Ava stood at the top of the stairs while Bastian stood in the main foyer with Gabe and Leo. Bastian nodded occasionally to his business partners, but it was easy to tell that he wasn't really listening to a word they had to say.

Ava took the first step and it was like watching a movie. As Bastian's head turned, his eyes widened and his mouth dropped at her beauty. The two of them glided together as if on magnets, their eyes bright and full of hope.

He met her at the bottom of the stairs and I saw her blush and say something. I was too far away to hear their conversation, but at least they were both smiling.

Bastian's hand moved through the air, and I knew he was going to draw her in for a kiss, except he paused and then stopped. His face went cold and his eyes distant.

I looked behind Ava to see Chad ruining my perfect romantic moment. This was not the happy reunion with kisses I had anticipated and it was all Chad's fault. I was *so* calling Eli.

Bastian's hand went back to his side and his eyes were guarded. Ava blushed and looked like she might faint at any moment. Which, given that I knew Bastian would catch her, wouldn't be the end of the world, but definitely not the moment I had imagined for them.

I took the first step of the stairs, determined to get my brother and my new friend their fairy tale moment, even if it meant killing the auctioneer before the auction. On the second step, Bastian clearly asked if they could go speak somewhere else and my hopes rose slightly.

I was paying more attention to where Bastian and Ava were going than I was to the stairs and tripped on the last step. Luckily, Leo was there to catch me. His hands were warm on my bare arms as he made sure I was steady before letting me go. I wished he had held on for just a moment longer.

"Thanks," I said, feeling a little silly for almost falling. My heart was pounding in my chest, and not just from nearly eating it. Leo looked amazing. His dark suit brought out the blue in his eyes and accented the strong lines of his shoulders and trim physique. Even his normally messy hair was brushed back and sleek. He looked every bit like a billionaire playboy and it had my body responding.

Damn him. I needed to concentrate on Bastian and Ava, not how good he looked in a suit. But, he just looked *so* good.

"What's up with them?" Leo asked, motioning toward the receding outline of Bastian and Ava as they headed toward the back porch and away from the party.

"Come with me," I said, grabbing his hand and pulling him along behind me as I followed my brother and his girlfriend. I needed to make sure they kissed and made up without that stupid auctioneer's words really ruining everything.

I realized I was still holding Leo's hand as we came to

the glass door leading out to the porch, and I quickly dropped my hand from his as we positioned ourselves to peek out on the couple. I was trying hard to keep my distance and not touch him. Touching Leo only let my heart hope for things it couldn't have.

The night was dark and the porch unlit, but there was still enough light for us to be able to watch. I pulled on the curtain, hiding us further from their sight.

We huddled together in the dark, peeking through the small space available to see, and I couldn't help but notice how he was pressed into me. Or was I pressed into him? Either way, we were touching and it was making it hard to think. I took a deep breath to try and center myself, but succeeded only in taking in his scent instead. Pure, clean and male. My heart skipped several beats before I could force it to start again.

"What's going on?" Leo asked again, a chuckle in his voice. His muscled arm was strong under his suit jacket as I held onto him in the dark. "What are we doing here?"

"It's a romantic reunion," I whispered back, trying my best to focus not on Leo and barely succeeding. Ten years of trying to ignore him helped, but it was hard with him this close.

Outside, Bastian was gripping the railing of the deck like he might tumble off the earth if he didn't hold on tight enough. Ava stood shaking in the pale moonlight with determination and fear on her face. I had promised her that he would welcome her back with open arms, and this wasn't exactly that.

"Damn it," I hissed as Bastian's shoulders hunched. "He should have just kissed her when he first saw her. This isn't how it is supposed to go!"

"Just being happy? Eh, that's not Bastian's style. He's got

to have the drama," Leo replied, peeking out at the two of them with me. "What do you think they're even talking about out there?"

I shrugged, but noticed that Bastian had perked up at whatever Ava was telling him. Maybe this could be the romantic, happy ending I had hoped for. "I don't know. Hopefully something wonderful."

I could feel Leo's eyes roll without even having to look at him. "You are such a hopeless romantic."

I gave him a gentle push with my hip, trying not to notice how solid he was in the process. "I like being a hopeless romantic, thank you very much."

Leo snickered and puffed up his chest. "Ava, I am a billionaire with a dark past, but I can't possibly look more handsome right now," Leo said in a deep voice that was meant to make fun of Bastian.

I giggled. He had Bastian down perfectly.

"Oh, Bastian," Leo continued, adopting a high, squeaky, feminine voice and tossing his head around like he had long hair. "You're absolutely right. The only man who could possibly look more handsome than you is Leo."

I smacked his arm, but giggled anyway. "Shh."

He grinned in the dark and reached for the door. I was afraid he was going to give us away, but the couple outside was too enraptured in one another to notice. The smell of fresh ocean and sand wafted into the house, mixing with the wonderful scent of Leo's cologne. Their voices were soft, but audible.

"Why are you here, Ava?" Bastian asked, his voice thrumming with hope. Ava took another step forward and touched his cheek. She traced the scar from his cheek bone down to the tip of his lips before speaking. Her love for him was obvious.

"I'm here because I had to tell you I love you." She smiled, and the truth of her words shone in her eyes brighter than moonlight. "I love you, Bastian."

Bastian didn't respond with words, he simply pulled her into him, kissing her like she was everything he had ever needed in his life. I couldn't help but blush at the sheer passion, but I knew a sappy smile was plastered across my face. This was the ending I wanted for them.

"I love you, too, Ava," Bastian replied, his voice rough with emotions. He bent to kiss her again and I grinned.

I wanted to whoop and jump for joy. My brother and my friend were happy. This was the moment I had wanted to create from the moment I saw Ava pull up in that cab. I grabbed Leo's arm and gave him a hug. He was so solid and strong beneath me that I let myself stay there for a moment. "It's perfect, Leo. That's love."

Leo frowned, his whole body still as he watched the reunion scene. "He really loves her, doesn't he?"

"Well, *yeah!*" I grinned up at him, still keeping my arms wrapped around him. "Isn't it great? They're so perfect for each other. You should see them together, Leo. It's honestly the happiest I've ever seen him. He smiles more and he isn't so damn angry all the time. He actually can control his temper now. He's *happy*. Like really, honestly joyful." I knew I was rambling, but I was just so giddy with their love. Bastian deserved someone as wonderful as Ava in his life.

"You really think they're going to last?" Leo asked, frowning as he continued to peer out the window. "I just remember the last time..."

I knew that Leo had been one of the major supports for Bastian the last time Bastian's heart had been broken. "You're a good friend to worry about him, Leo." I looked out, reveling in the warm glow that surrounded the lovers. It brought tears to my eyes. "But, yes. I do. I really, really do. I've never seen anything like the two of them. It's basically magic."

"Magic, huh?" Leo asked, turning to look at me. I realized I was still snuggled up and holding onto his arm. I released my grip on him go with a blush. Leo's eyes were dark and I could see thoughts running through them. He was probably just thinking of his friendship with Bastian and how it would change with a new girl in the picture.

I went back to looking out the window at the happy couple, wrapping my arms around myself. I was just so glad to see two people I cared about getting their happy ending. I was glad it was Leo here sharing it with me. Of all the people in the world, I wanted to share a moment like this with him.

He was still close enough for me to be able to feel his warmth. The air conditioning was running at full blast inside the house, so his heat was a welcome respite from the cool. I wished I could cuddle up into him and soak the heat from him directly. My chest squeezed with longing, my heart aching for more of Leo than I could ever have.

"Charlotte..." My name came out heavy like honey on Leo's voice. The way he said it sent pleasurable shivers down my spine. It was how I always wanted him to say my name right before he kissed me.

I turned, expecting to see Leo looking at me the way Bastian was looking at Ava, hopefully as caught up in the magic of their love as I was, but kinstead I found him looking at the event coordinator hurrying down the hallway.

"There you are!" the woman called out gratefully, stopping whatever Leo was going to say next. She hurried up to the two of us, barely giving our strange position behind the curtain a second glance. "Do you know where Mr. Belrose is? It's time for his speech. The champagne is being passed out. There isn't much time."

"Thank you, I'll let him know," I replied, rising from my spot and smoothing my dress. I hoped she didn't think we were peeping toms. I just wanted to make sure that my brother and my friend got the happy ever after they deserved.

The woman nodded and hurried back toward the sounds of the party. With a sigh, I looked over at Leo. "Were you going to say something?"

"It can wait." He shook his head with a sad smile that made me curious. He probably just had some droll comment about me being a hopeless romantic. "Go get him for his speech. He worked hard for it."

I grinned at him and went to the door.

"I'm sorry to interrupt," I announced stepping outside. I grinned at the two of them, even though I was obviously interrupting their kiss. "But it's time for your speech, Bastian."

Bastian grinned at the beautiful woman in his arms. "Come with me."

She willingly took his arm as he escorted her inside. I held up my hand and gave them both high-fives as they passed. The two of them walked with a happy glow surrounding them that I couldn't help but envy as I held the door open. I'd never seen my brother look so happy, and that filled my heart with joy.

Once they were off the porch, I came inside to follow them. I got two steps down the hall before Leo grabbed my hand.

"Come with me." It wasn't a question or a demand.

"But the speech..." I stammered, feeling a new heat in his

gaze as he looked at me. Something had changed in his eyes, but I wasn't sure what.

"You know what he's going to say," Leo said, giving me a gentle tug back toward the moonlit porch. "Do you really need to hear it?"

I paused for a moment, looking after the happy couple and then back to Leo. His hand was still on mine and I didn't want him to let go. Ever.

"Okay," I whispered, just happy to have him with me.

6

Leo still had my hand wrapped up in his and it was doing strange things to my heart. He'd never touched me for this long, at least not on purpose. With every moment, I knew I was falling just a little more in love with him and that I would crave his touch for days after this. It was almost cruel to know I wouldn't get it.

Outside on the porch, the night was calm and beautiful. A cooling wind came in from the ocean, bringing the scent of salt and sand with it. The waning moon's small crescent shape was a silver glitter against the dark water of the Caribbean sea.

Just before Leo closed the door, I heard the soft rumble of applause as Bastian began his speech inside. The door sealed with a soft thud, separating Leo and me from the rest of the world. It was warm and dark out here, and still thrumming with the magic of Bastian and Ava's reunion. I wanted to be in a world with just Leo, even if it was only for a moment. Even if I couldn't really have him, I wanted this moment.

"Charlotte?"

I loved the way my name sounded on his lips. I smiled, slowly turning to face him in the dark. My pulse fluttered along the pulse points of wrists and along my neck the way it always did whenever Leo was close. He smiled, reaching for my face with his hand. Everything slowed and moved in slow-motion as he reached for me and then pulled me into a kiss. It was every dream I'd ever had come true.

His hands cradled my face as he pressed his lips against mine, our mouths searching and seeking for more. In his hands and pressed against his lips, I was his. He was claiming me as his own and making my heart soar for it. My fantasies had never done this first kiss justice.

I was breathing hard when he pulled back, his hands still on my face as his eyes searched my face. I knew I must have fallen and bumped my head and was dreaming, or that I was possibly dead- because this was heaven. Even though I had written our love story a thousand times in my head, I never once thought it would happen.

Leo kissed me.

"I've wanted to do that for years now," he whispered with a grin as his eyes found mine. I had to be dreaming. There was no way for a human being to feel this happy after just one kiss. I didn't know why he was suddenly kissing me after all these years, but I didn't care. I just wanted to kiss him again and again and again.

"You wanted to kiss me?" I gasped, having trouble forming words after such an amazing kiss. "Really?"

Leo leaned in closer, tipping his forehead to mine. "It was even better than I thought possible."

I couldn't stop myself from reaching up and pulling him in for another kiss before he could barely finish his sentence. If this was a dream, I was going to kiss him until I woke up. I prayed that I would never wake up from this. Kissing him felt so right.

"I've wanted to kiss *you* for years," I finally said, needing to say the words. "I even asked!" I looked up at him, seeing the blue in his eyes even in the moonlight. He was so damn good looking I could barely stand it. I fit in his arms like a puzzle piece.

I didn't want to ask, but I knew I needed to. I was afraid that if I asked, I would break the spell and Leo would realize who he was kissing and would leave. But I had to know. "Why now?"

"Because Bastian has someone," he said as if it were the most logical thing in the world.

"What? That makes no sense," I replied, shaking my head. "Whether or not my brother has someone shouldn't determine if you're kissing me."

Leo's eyes met mine and one side of his mouth quirked into a smile as he shrugged. "I always thought you and Bastian would end up together."

I couldn't help it. I snorted. The idea of me and Bastian was utterly ridiculous. "You thought I'd end up with Bastian?"

"I'm serious," he insisted. I loved the way his arms were still wrapped around me, keeping me pressed into the strength of his chest. "I thought you two were supposed to be together. You're good together. He obviously respects and loves you. I just thought that it would be the natural outcome. I didn't want to ruin a good thing."

"Leo, he's my brother. In every sense of the word except the genetic one. We grew up as siblings." I shook my head. For someone as smart as Leo, that reason was rather dumb. Sweet, but dumb. "If I had known that was what was stopping you all this time..."

Leo brushed hair away from my face and sent my world spinning with the tender touch. Other than finding out we had never done this because he thought I should end up with my brother, this kiss was everything I had ever dreamed it could be. Yet, it still didn't feel real.

"But why now?" I pressed. "Bastian's had girlfriends before. There has to be more of a reason than just Bastian."

Leo bent his head and kissed me again. His kiss stole all of my ability to think, sending me soaring to another, happier plane of being. I completely lost my train of thought as Leo kissed me, and damn if he wasn't an even better kisser than I had imagined.

"Why?" I finally gasped, unwilling to let him get off with just a kiss. I needed to know. I needed to know this wasn't just out of pity or if it was just going to be a one-time thing. I would take a one-time thing, I would take anything from Leo, but I needed to know so I wouldn't get hurt.

He stopped kissing me long enough to grin. "Because I don't want to wait anymore. I'm done waiting. I needed to kiss you, at least once."

"Just once?" My heart stalled a little. I wanted to kiss him far more than just once. Billions of kisses wouldn't be enough.

"*At least* once," he clarified, bending his head to mine again. "But I'm not sure that even a million would satisfy me now."

"Ms. Page!" An urgent cry came as the door opened and interrupted my perfect night. Standing in the doorway was the party coordinator, looking incredibly flustered. Her hair was mussed and her cheeks red.

"Yes?" I asked, trying very hard not to be annoyed. She had no way of knowing what she was interrupting. Well, maybe she did since she found us hiding in the curtain earlier.

"I'm very sorry to interrupt, but I'm afraid there's a problem in the kitchen and it can't wait." She then turned to Leo. "Also, Mr. Westbrook, Mr. Belrose is looking for you."

"Of course he is," Leo said under his breath. He still kept his hold on me.

"Ms. Page, it really is important," she stuttered, obviously not willing to leave the porch without me.

I sighed. The last thing in the entire world that I wanted to do was leave Leo's arms. But duty called. My fantasies would have to wait. Next time, though, I was locking that door.

Leo reluctantly let me go. I took a step to the door before turning to look back at him. He was so handsome that my heart might explode out of my chest with joy. He had kissed me. That man with the beautiful hair and stunning eyes, that made me laugh and smile, had kissed me. He looked as flushed and pleased as I did, yet still managing to pull of debonair and smooth as well.

"I still get that dance, right?" I asked, stopping despite the coordinator's anxious movements.

Leo grinned. "I'm counting on it."

Butterflies danced and soared in my stomach and I was light headed and just a little giddy. I would go take care of this kitchen thing in two seconds so I could come back to this. To have him kiss me again. Dance with me.

With one last grin, I turned and hurried after the party coordinator, leaving the love of my life smiling at me on the porch.

7

———

The kitchen was on fire.

Or at least, it had been.

The acrid scent of smoke lingered in the kitchen despite the open windows and the industrial fan sucking up as much of it as possible. Luckily, the scent had remained contained and wasn't frightening the guests.

The chicken however, was very frightening.

"I'm so sorry Ms. Page- the chicken flambé, it wasn't supposed to do that!" The poor caterer looked to be about two seconds away from bursting into tears. This was probably one of the biggest events on the island, and definitely not how she had planned on making an impression on our guests. "I've done this a thousand times and-"

"Are you okay?" I cut her off, putting my hands on her shoulders. "Are you or any of your staff hurt?"

"I'm okay, the staff is okay," she sniffled, not meeting my eyes. I could smell the scent of burnt hair lingering around her, and upon closer inspection noticed her eyebrows were singed. A single tear rolled down her flushed cheeks. "But the dinner isn't."

I took a closer look at the charcoal mess of meat beneath the smoke hood. It looked more like lava than chicken, and there was no way it was even close to edible. I had no idea that chicken was that flammable.

"It's not the end of the world," I said, following the line of singed paint up the wall to the slightly melted ceiling. Bastian was going to be pissed that his beloved kitchen looked like this. It was a good thing we were selling this mansion and that Ava was here to mellow him out. I sighed. "Do we have more somewhere?"

The caterer shook her head no, her chin quivering as she dry-washed her hands.

"Okay." I thought for a moment. This was my job. I solved problems before they ever got to Bastian, and burnt chicken was possibly one of the easier ones I'd ever faced. I turned to the party coordinator. "Inform everyone that the chicken dish has changed and there will be a slight delay."

The party coordinator nodded. "Luckily, nothing but appetizers have been served so far, so at least no one is waiting for food."

I nodded and pulled out my phone, hitting my favorite speed dial while on the island. "Hello? Adele's Restaurant? I need to place an order of Maria's Special Chicken."

Luckily, I was on very good terms with the owner and chef of the cute little local restaurant. If anyone would have enough food fit for a party, it would be Adele's.

The voice on the other line told me I was in luck. Since we were the main event on the island tonight, business was slow and they happened to have a batch of chicken already prepared. They could be here in twenty minutes.

Thanking my lucky stars, I gave them a few more details and told them to put it on my tab. I let out a little sigh of relief as I hung up the phone and slipped it back into my pocket. Crisis averted.

"The chicken replacement will be here in twenty. Is there anything else that needs to be cooked?" I asked the caterer.

"Really, the flambé was the last step and I've never seen flambé do that before," she answered, her voice slowly gaining strength. For the last ten minutes she had most likely been terrified for her business. A mistake of this size, no matter how accidental, would have ruined her. "All the other main dishes are either on the grill or already cooked... except dessert."

"What's dessert?" I racked my brain, but I had finalized the menu months ago and couldn't remember what Bastian and I had settled on. I just remembered that it had been delicious and the reason we had picked her to cater the meal.

"Baked Alaska and crème brulee."

Of course. Two dishes that required fire.

"Are you up for it?" I asked, taking in her scorched appearance. She seemed to be calming down and getting herself back together, but I could imagine that she would want to be a little leery of fire after the chicken incident.

"I think so." She swallowed hard and her hand unconsciously went to her scorched hair. "It's all table-side, so as long as I don't light the guests on fire, it'll be fine."

"Okay then," I replied, smiling at her attempt at humor. "Then everything is fine."

"I'll pay for the chicken, Ms. Page," the caterer said. Her eyes were bright. "No matter what happened, the food is my responsibility."

"That sounds fair," I replied.

"Thank you," the caterer said breathlessly. "This event is

the opportunity of a lifetime. Thank you for understanding."

"Accidents happen," I said with a shrug. "Lord knows I've done worse things to chicken."

There was a very good reason Bastian cooked and not me. I could burn water.

The party coordinator came back into the kitchen. I turned to her. "The chicken will be here in twenty minutes."

"Excellent." The coordinator let out a sigh of relief. "I can handle the rest of the meal as planned then."

"Good." I smiled at the other two women, glad this had been a relatively easy fix. "Please inform me of any other problems. I'm going back to the party to mingle with Mr. Belrose's guests."

And Leo, I told myself silently. And Leo.

8

Everyone was seated in the party tents to the back of the mansion. Despite the massive size of the mansion, there just wasn't a good place to seat one-hundred and fifty for a formal setting. Especially not with the unparalleled view of the ocean that the tents offered. Tomorrow, these tents would be used for some of the smaller, more durable pieces being auctioned off.

White linen and stringed lights gave the dinner a very Caribbean flavor that managed to look both comfortable and elegant at the same time, especially with the perfect ocean view. The tent doors were open to allow in the breeze, but the steady hum of the air conditioners kept the room comfortable. Camera flashes went off at regular intervals as the rich and powerful mingled over cocktails and appetizers.

I immediately located Bastian, Gabe, and Leo all sitting at the head table. Ava sat next to Bastian, positively glowing with happiness. There was an empty chair next to her and the final two seats contained two friends, Jack and Emma Saunders.

Emma laughed, her dark hair piled on top of her head in a glorious crown of curls while her billionaire oil-baron husband, Jack, looked on adoringly. I had hoped the two of them would come to our gala and auction, as they were billionaires and had a connection to the island. In fact, it had been Jack that had told Bastain about this undiscovered paradise before he bought the house here. Two years ago, they met on the beach just south of here and fell head over heels in love. It was a love story I loved watching unfold a little more every time I saw them.

"There you are," Bastian greeted me, rising from the table as soon as he saw me. Several flashbulbs went off behind me and I knew the billionaires' table, not the woman singing on stage, was the center of attention.

I took my seat between Ava and Emma and all four men stood in an attempt to be formal. It made me laugh as Gabe, Leo, and Bastian were perhaps the least formal men I knew. Most evenings, the three of them just sat on a couch eating pizza in sweats. Jack had grown up with money, but even then, it felt strange. It was something that I certainly had never gotten used to living with the upper crust.

Leo sat across from me at the table. Our eyes met and he grinned. All I wanted to do was talk to him, to make sure that the kiss we shared on the porch was actually real and not just a part of my over-active imagination.

Unfortunately, sitting at a table with my overprotective big brother and a host of photographers just hoping for the next big news break was not the place to talk, let alone make out.

"Bastian," Jack said as our salads arrived. "This is an amazing thing you're doing here."

"Thank you," Bastian graciously accepted. I stared down the pretty arugula salad, not wanting to eat. I wanted to kiss

Leo, not munch on rabbit food. Unfortunately, there wasn't an easy way to get out of dinner. Perhaps, after dinner I could pull him aside for a moment...

"I plan on bidding on several items tomorrow just to support your cause," Jack continued. "But, I don't think I've ever actually heard the full story as to how you got here. To be honest, I didn't even know you were in the foster system. You've managed to keep yourself out of the limelight."

Bastian took a sip of his wine. "That was intentional. As I recall, the limelight nearly destroyed you and Emma not too long ago."

Emma chuckled. "Well, I'd say it brought us together, even if it wasn't entirely planned that way."

Bastian nodded and set down his glass. "For a long time, I kept my past a secret. I couldn't keep the car accident a secret since it was in the papers, but I kept what happened to me after quiet. The foster system was rough. I got lucky and had a good family, and I then I got Charlotte."

Bastian paused to smile at me warmly. If anything, I was the lucky one. I got Bastian.

"We had a good family, but a lot of kids fall through the cracks." Bastian looked around at everyone at the table, his passion vibrating through every word. "There are kids who have been in the system since they were little and don't know what a family should be. There are a lot of very dark things that occur in the world."

I stared at my salad. I knew that the world was dark better than most, and I still considered myself lucky. I'd put my past behind me as much as Bastian had. My parents weren't my family. Bastian was. He was the only person who had always been there for me, even after Leo started looking after me as well.

Thinking of Leo and Bastian made me remember Leo's

crazy idea that Bastian and I would end up together. On the one hand, I could see how he might come to that conclusion. Bastian and I had always been close, and he wasn't the first to make the assumption that since we weren't biologically related, falling in love was the next logical step.

Except, Bastian and I were broken the same way. We shared the same cracks in our armor and similar defense mechanisms. For a romantic relationship to work, for two people to connect on the level needed for that kind of love, they couldn't be the same. Our armor would clash and we'd fall apart.

And besides that, Bastian was just *Bastian*. Ugh.

"Yet, here you are with a billion-dollar corporation. It speaks to your strength," Jack was saying. I tried to focus back into the conversation. It was hard with Leo literally right in front of me but with no real way to talk to him. So close and yet so far.

"Thank you, but I think it speaks to my friends more," Bastian said with an easy smile. He grinned at the other two men sitting at the table. "Without Gabe and Leo, there would be no business. Without Charlotte, we would have been lost in all the details."

"Okay, so I love a good origin story and this sounds like it is one," Emma jumped in. Her dark eyes were bright and interested. She wasn't the typical Hollywood beauty or even model pretty, but she was still stunning. She was real and that made her beautiful. It was easy to see why Jack had fallen so hard for her. "How did you get Kindling Dating started?"

"Let me, I love telling this story," Gabe offered. Bastian and Leo both rolled their eyes. Gabe loved attention, especially from pretty ladies. Even if they were married.

"Go ahead," Bastian said, leaning back in his chair. I

looked over at Gabe, interested to hear yet another one of his infamous versions of how integral he was to starting the business. The last one had him basically creating everything from scratch all by himself.

"It was all my idea," Gabe began. Leo made a soft snort and I giggled. He glared at both of us before continuing. "Bastian here had just gotten his heart stomped on. I felt for the guy and wanted to set him up with a girl who wouldn't break his heart."

"That's the story you're going with this time?" Leo teased. "Not the finding an easy way to get laid side of the story?"

Gabe ignored him. "So, being *such* a good friend, I started looking around and realized that we had an opportunity. There was no good way to sort potential dates on the market, so we made one."

It was then that our dinners arrived. I had ordered the chicken and was pleased to see that it was perfect. All the other tables were going quiet as everyone started to dig into the delicious food. I took a bite, savoring the succulent breast combining with Caribbean flavors and heat. Jerk spices, mixed with some sort of sweetness that made the heat tolerable rolled across my tongue. It was hard not to snarf the entire thing in one bite.

"Anyway," Gabe continued once the servers moved on to the next table. "We built the core business together, and then focused on our strengths. Bastian figured out how to make it all work, I did the marketing, and Leo was our money guy." He took a bite of his steak, making a pleased face before swallowing. He put his hand on Leo's shoulder. "Actually, Leo deserves a lot of praise. I don't know how he did it, but he got us a sweetheart deal on a loan. Enough for us to really get going. I don't know if we would be where we are without those start-up funds."

Leo turned bright red and nearly choked on his chicken dinner. "It really wasn't that important-" he stuttered.

"It saved our asses, Leo," Gabe insisted. "Don't be modest." Gabe looked around the table with smile. "And that was the beginning. Everything just kind of snowballed from there and the next thing you know, we're sitting at the billionaire's table."

"Don't forget Charlotte in your story, Gabe," Leo reminded him. I blushed as Leo grinned at me. Leo always had to make me feel special.

Gabe swallowed his bite of food. "Of course! Charlotte here was our first employee. She's the one who made sure we all stayed sane by doing all the paperwork and making sure we made it to meetings on time." He paused for dramatic effect and then in a loud stage whisper added, "Don't tell her, but she was kind of important. I don't want her to know her nerd skills were actually kind of useful."

I laughed. "I really just wanted to show these guys they were wrong." I turned to Emma. "They used to tease me about taking accounting classes in high school. Called me a numbers nerd."

"You still are a numbers nerd," Leo teased gently. His blue eyes sparkled at me from across the table, knowing that this was something that always got me riled. It took every-thing not to retort back that he had just kissed a numbers nerd and liked it.

Not appropriate dinner conversation, I reminded myself. Not to mention that Bastian would probably get up and punch him on principle. I was still his little sister, even if Leo was his friend.

"How *did* you get that loan?" I asked, trying to deflect the conversation away from me. "I remember writing the checks for the interest payments and wondering how you got such a good interest rate for us. I couldn't find anything close at any of the banks I tried."

Leo turned on his business smile. I had learned that every businessman had one and that when they wore it, they couldn't be trusted. Even Leo.

"That's my business secret and I can't give them all away," he replied, the smile never faltering. He turned to Jack and Emma. "But, now Jack, how is it being back on the island? I know that you met your lovely wife Emma here. Are you two staying at that resort again or somewhere else on the island?"

I frowned slightly at the sudden change in topic, but let it slide. The loan was five years ago. It wasn't something I needed to press, especially if it made Leo uncomfortable. I had always secretly suspected that he had asked a wealthy relative or done something similarly embarrassing to help us all succeed.

"We're staying at the resort for nostalgia's sake," Jack said, taking Emma's hand in his. His eyes lit up with a love that made me weak in the knees as he looked at her. "I think it's even better the second time."

It was all I could do not to let out a huge, *"Awww!"* I glanced back and forth between Jack and Emma to Bastian and Ava. Love was sweet, and looking across the table at the man with the blue eyes, I couldn't wait to find out just how sweet it could be.

Leo grinned and pushed back his seat, apparently thinking along the same lines. He sidestepped the waitress picking up dishes who Gabe was busy flirting with to come over to me. He held out his hand. "While we wait for dessert, would you like to dance?"

"I'd love to," I replied honestly. He wrapped my smaller hand in his. I hoped he couldn't feel my heart pounding through my skin. I wanted so much more than a dance, but if a dance was all I could get right now, I would take it.

Leo led me to the open dance floor, spinning me expertly into the music as a fresh song began. I fit into his arms like I was made there. Leo was an excellent dancer and following his lead into a waltz was easier than breathing. Cameras flashed and zinged as we danced, and as I looked up at my prince charming, I felt like a princess.

"So?" I looked up at him, half expecting him to tell me it was all a mistake, or even worse, that I would wake up and find this all a dream.

"So." He grinned at me and spun me around, making my skirt flow out in a shimmer of blue fabric before pulling me back into the safety of his arms. "I wish we could get out of here. I'd like to kiss you some more, but-"

A camera flash interrupted his words and accenting how public our setting was.

"-But the auction should be front page news. Not us," he finished, spinning me away from the camera. "I'll just have to be content with holding you until later. Then I want to kiss you again. And again."

Happy bubbles filled my chest and if it was possible for a person to die of happiness, I was certainly close. Leo wanted to kiss me again. He wanted me. My willpower was going to be severely depleted by the end of the night. All I wanted to do was pull him off the dance floor into a dark corner and have my way with him.

I sighed. The gala would go on for hours. There was time for that later. I'd waited ten years for this. I could wait a couple more hours.

"Is there anything you're bidding on at the auction

tomorrow?" I asked, trying to distract myself from how close his lips were and how good he smelled.

"Small talk, huh?" He tipped his head just enough that I could see the beginning of a kiss and I held my breath. "Good plan. Yes, there are several things I plan on purchasing."

The song ended and a round of applause surrounded us for dancing.

"Another, please?" I asked, not wanting to go back to the table just yet. If I couldn't kiss him, at least I could be in his arms.

"How much work do you have to do tomorrow? I'd like to see you," Leo said, twirling me to the music. Several more couples joined us on the dance floor.

"I have to help during the day. Once the auction is complete, the auction house will take care of everything and I'll be done." I sighed. "I can't wait. I believe in this auction so much, but it has been a lot of work."

"You've done a fantastic job," Leo murmured, taking us to the corner of the dance floor and out of limelight. The other dancers would keep the photographers' attention as long as we didn't do anything too out of the ordinary.

"Thank you," I said, flushing with pride. It was one thing for my brother to tell me I had done well, but Leo saying it made it feel real. "Are you doing anything other than the auction tomorrow?"

"I was planning on taking my boat out and enjoying the island for a bit. The items I want aren't on sale until the end of the auction anyway," Leo explained.

I paused. "Which boat?" There was a boat of his that I did not like. A dangerous boat. I sincerely hoped he meant his yacht or a sailboat. Or even a paddle-boat. Anything but his racing boat.

"The one you hate," he teased, confirming what I was dreading.

"I hate it because it's dangerous, Leo." My happy feelings were quickly disappearing. I felt a little cold, even despite the warm Caribbean air. That boat was bad news.

"You're just a worry-wart," Leo started. This was a familiar argument. One we'd had at least a hundred times before. He usually just stepped around me and did whatever he pleased, but I wasn't going to let it slide. Not this time. Not when he said he wanted to kiss me.

"I worry because I care!" I stopped dancing and stepped away from him. "Your boat was designed to break the water speed record. A record with an eighty-five percent fatality rate, Leo. No sane person takes those odds."

I hated even thinking about it. The water speed record was the fastest a boat had ever gone. There was a good reason why no one had beaten the record of 317mph set in 1978- everyone who tried usually ended up dead on the water. Going speeds that fast, the water turned into cement and the smallest wave, a stray piece of kelp, or a moment's distraction could send the boat hydroplaning into the water. With a fatality rate of eighty-five percent since 1940, trying to break the water speed record was a death wish. Yet, Leo insisted on playing with the boats capable of doing it.

He picked my hands back up and spun me back into the dance. "I'm still here, aren't I?"

"That's not the point," I said, a scowl filling my face. My steps back into the dance were slow and unwilling. "It's dangerous."

Leo sighed. "Charlotte, I'm not racing. I go out, I get some speed, and I come back in. I'm not trying to break the water speed record. I'm just enjoying the boat."

"A boat that is designed to break records. It's not exactly

a normal speed boat." I paused, hating the sinking feeling thinking of his boat always gave me. "I've seen you crash on the water, Leo. The last one put you in the hospital."

"For a day, Charlotte," Leo snapped, getting frustrated. He spun me around, but the motion was angry rather than graceful. "And the doctor said that was overkill. I'm fine. You can tell Bastian not to go out on the water, but not me."

I thought of how Bastian went out paddle-boarding every morning and how I would get so angry at finding his broken boards or other evidence of him being dangerous out on the water. Bastian, Leo and Gabe were my only family. If anything happened to them...

"Do you know why I ask him not to go out?" I asked quietly. My feet shuffled to the music, not really dancing. I couldn't meet his eyes and instead stared at his suit jacket. He had a dark gray handkerchief in his pocket folded into an elaborate design. "I don't care that he's paddle boarding. I don't even care about the sharks or the rogue waves or what could happen. I ask him because I'm selfish."

"Selfish?" Leo asked, surprise filling his voice. His step faltered. "You are one of the least selfish people I know. You put your life on hold for this auction, even though it's Bastian's." He stopped dancing and put his hand under my chin, gently forcing me to look up at him. "Why, Charlotte? Why do you ask him not to push the limits when it's what the three of us were born to do?"

The memory, the nightmare, flashed to my memory.

I wake up from my nap to see the neighbor lady slowly getting up from the raggedy chair by the TV. Someone is knocking on the door.

It's a police officer, his uniform wet with rain. He says something to the old woman. She smells like cats, but she's the only one who can watch me when Mommy and Daddy have to leave. I hate when they're gone. They always come back smelling strange.

The old woman covers her mouth with her hand and looks over at me.

There's terror and heartbreak in her eyes that I don't yet understand.

But I will.

"It's because I can't lose him," I whisper, avoiding Leo's eyes. "Bastian is my foster brother because I lost everyone when I was six years old. They left one night, and never came back." There was more to it than that. It was complicated and something I wasn't proud of, but the truth was still there. I slowly raised my eyes to meet his. "I don't want to lose you, too. Not to some stupid boat."

Leo's blue eyes softened and his expression shifted from exasperation to concern. "You've never told me that part," he said softly. His hands went to my shoulders and he kissed my forehead. "Okay."

"Okay, what?" Tears were trying to form in my eyes at the memory of being alone. I never wanted to be alone like that again. I was glad there were several other couples on the dance floor so we weren't just standing there with me about to burst into tears.

"Okay, I won't go out on the boat. For you." He pulled me in close, his arms wrapping around me and keeping me safe. "Because I care about you, too."

"Really?" My voice was muffled by his suit jacket as I pressed my face into his chest, not caring if I smudged my mascara on it.

"I kissed you today, didn't I?" he said softly. He looked down, a soft smile filling his handsome face. "And all I want to do is kiss you again."

I smiled back, blinking the tears out of my eyes. "Me too."

I nestled into his shoulder, letting him hug me more than dance. With his arms around me, I was safe. The nightmare memory faded until it was just static in the back of my mind. Leo wouldn't leave me. He never had, and he never would.

The song ended and another round of applause scattered through the tent as the new dancers took their bows.

"More," I demanded, knowing I sounded like a petulant child. I wasn't ready to leave his arms yet.

Leo sighed. "Unfortunately, dessert is here, and Bastian looks like he's slightly concerned about what I'm doing to you."

"That's because your hand is on my ass," I informed him.

"Do you have a problem with that?" he asked.

"Nope," I replied with a naughty grin. "In fact, I encourage it."

"Just you wait." He grinned back at me for a moment before releasing me and offering me his arm to take me back to the table. "I have some other ideas you might encourage."

9

———

Leo reluctantly let go of my arm to pull out my chair for me. I tried not to shiver as he brushed his hand along the bare skin of my back as he left to take his own seat. Heat built in my core at the slightest of his touches.

In the center of the table was a beautiful bowl full of meringue covered ice cream. The caterer gave me a nervous smile as she cut an orange peel into a long thin string. After pouring liquor on the meringue, she dipped the string of orange peel into a saucer of Grand Marnier. With a deep breath, she lit the orange peel on fire.

The sweet scent of alcohol and orange filled the tent as she set the pretty dessert danced with blue and orange flames. The caterer carefully made sure nothing burned, definitely hyper-aware of the danger of the flames. It was a beautiful dessert and as the flames slowly died, the scent of sugar hit me.

The caterer let out a small sigh of relief as everyone clapped. She grinned at me before carefully placing seven small cups of perfect crème brulee on a serving plate and hurrying off to the next table.

Bastian scooped the ice cream, cake, and meringue concoction onto plates. The sweet scent of orange still lingered as I took a bite. It was a delicious mixture of hot and cold mingled with wonderful sweetness. This was why we had hired the caterer. It was absolutely divine.

The table fell silent for a moment as everyone tasted their desserts. The Baked Alaska was perfect and the crème brulee thick and creamy, yet with the perfect sugar shell crunch characteristic of the dish. It was almost as good as kissing Leo.

Almost.

It was painful to have him sitting across the table, yet not be able to touch him. Beside me, Ava and Bastian were holding hands. I wanted to do that with Leo. On my other side, Emma and Jack were gazing at one another with adoration. I wanted to do that, too.

But I had to sit, staring at the man of my dreams, knowing that we could be off kissing somewhere and being unable to do it. For the first time in my life, I hated my job. I hated that we had to have a public face and that the cameras were always watching.

Knowing that I could have everything my heart desired, that Leo wanted me and that we had to sit here and make polite conversation, was torture. All I wanted to do was kiss him again. I wanted my love story to begin.

Leo's phone started to ring. He patted his pocket, turning it off and looking embarrassed. "I told Toby not to bother me unless it's an emergency. Please excuse me."

With a smooth motion and a pleasant smile, he stood from the table and put the phone to his ear. He said something into the mouthpiece as he navigated away from the noise of the tables and to the far corner of the tent.

I tried to pay attention to Emma as she described the adorable antics of her niece, but I couldn't. My eyes just kept going back to where Leo had disappeared out of the tent. I wanted him to come back to the table and laugh along with me. I wanted another dance, and I desperately wanted to end the evening walking back with him.

It wasn't that I didn't enjoy the party. Any other night, I would have been ecstatic for the opportunity to giggle with Ava and Emma, to dance with my brother and Gabe, and to enjoy the food.

But Leo had kissed me tonight. And now, that's all I could think about.

Movement at the edge of the tent caught my eye. Leo was coming back.

I held my breath for a moment, waiting for him to return. He paused at the edge of the tent. His face was pale and the whites of his eyes were huge. He wiped sweat from his brow, despite the fact the air conditioners were keeping the room almost chilly. I'd never seen him look so shaken. He was always the epitome of cool and calm. Something unpleasant had happened in that phone call. He looked up and our eyes met.

He froze. I smiled, hoping he would return to his easy smile and laughing eyes. He licked his lips and his brow darkened. Instead of smiling back, he shook his head and tapped his phone.

Bing. A new text.

I carefully pulled my phone out of my dress and read his message.

Can't stay. Eat my dessert for me. I'll see you tomorrow at the auction. You did great today, and I want to kiss you again.

I frowned, confused at the message. He wanted to kiss me again, but he was leaving? I didn't understand. When I looked up, Leo was gone. The only indication he had ever been there was the tent door slowly fluttering to a standstill.

I didn't want any more dessert. The idea of eating actually made me a little queasy. What was wrong with Leo? Was he having second thoughts about us? Why else would he leave? I glanced back down at my phone, searching for a better answer as to why he had left. Unfortunately, I couldn't come up with one. Whatever that phone call was about, it was important enough for him to leave.

I hoped it wasn't me.

For a moment, I considered getting up from the table and going to look for him. He couldn't have gotten far and he was most likely headed back to the place he was renting on the island. I set my napkin down on the table, determined to find out what was so important to Leo that he would ditch out on an important dinner like this.

"You okay, Charlotte?" Gabe asked, cutting into my thoughts. "You look worried."

I looked up at Gabe. I had practically grown up with him since he moved in next door to my foster family. He and Bastian and been inseparable as kids and his little sister was my closest girlfriend.

"I'm fine," I said, putting the phone back in my pocket. "Just trying to figure out why Leo left."

"Don't worry about Leo. It's his loss for leaving." Gabe stood from the table and moved to offer me his hand. "Besides, it's my turn for a dance."

I wanted to chase after Leo, but I had responsibilities here. It would be noticed if Bastian's sister and assistant disappeared. I had done just as much as Bastian had to make this gala and auction happen and it would be odd for me to leave. A flashbulb went off as yet another photographer took my picture.

I patted my phone back in my pocket, checking that it was secure. I would be able to feel if it vibrated with Leo changing his mind. I glanced one last time at the tent door and then around at the party. I couldn't leave. Not really.

I had responsibilities. Besides, Leo probably had a good reason. He always did. Leo was the most dependable person I knew. He'd helped me out more times than I could count, and I knew he had done the same for others.

One of his friends must need help, I thought to myself. *Yes, that made sense. Leo was just helping someone.* I didn't know if it was true or not, but it made me feel better. I remembered how he had helped me study for a test I was sure I was going to fail and I knew that I was right. Leo wouldn't leave without a good reason.

I tried to smile and be happy. Leo was probably saving the world. I could stay here and smile for the photographers and do my part to make the gala a success.

Taking Gabe's hand was easy, but I still wished it was Leo's hand instead. As a consolation prize, Gabe was an even better dancer than Leo was. As he twirled me around, I decided to have fun tonight, even if I couldn't go chase after Leo. It was really the only thing I could do.

Another camera flash went off and I knew I had made the right decision to stay.

Besides, I'd see him tomorrow. After he was done helping his friend, just as he had helped me that night...

10

———————

3 Years Ago

"I'M GOING TO FAIL, LEO."

"You are not going to fail," he promised, sitting down at the table across from me. He looked wonderfully handsome in his dress shirt and slacks. "You are going to ace this test and graduate with honors."

I banged my head on the book in front of me, wishing I could just absorb the information that way. Damn Professor Blanks and his stupid final. This was the last class I needed to graduate, but due to my work schedule, I hadn't gone to very many classes. It hadn't seemed like a big problem since it was supposed to be an easy course to meet my English requirement.

Except it hadn't been that easy, and now I was paying the price. The Theory of Literature wasn't exactly something I could ingest overnight. Numbers, business, and accounting all made sense in my head, but the finer points of literature were a bit more tricky. It was so subjective that my objective brain rebelled even thinking about it.

"No, seriously, Leo- I'm never going to get this." I banged my head again. "I'm sorry I called you. You should go on your date."

Leo reached out and took my hand. I kept my head on my book, trying desperately to ignore the electricity running through me at his simple touch. He didn't feel that way about me, no matter how much I wished he did.

I was his friend's little sister. A friend. Nothing more. That's all I'd ever be.

My brain realized this, but my heart and body just hadn't gotten that memo yet.

"Charlotte," he said softly. "I believe in you. You can do this. You've managed to help us set up Kindling and get all your course work done. You're amazing. Don't let this one test stop you."

My chest squeezed hard on my heart. I wanted to believe Leo.

"I just..." I raised my head and looked at the book in front of me. It looked more like gibberish than actual words. "How am I going to learn all this in one night?"

"I'm going to help you." Leo said it without hesitation. "I even brought energy drinks and flashcards."

I looked up at him. He was serious. Those blue eyes were smiling at me, but they were serious. "Really?"

"You called me and said you needed help." Leo handed me an energy drink. "I'll stay here all night if you need me to. You're going to pass this test, Charlotte."

"Okay." I sighed. If Leo thought I could do it, then I could do it. I still felt guilty for taking him away from his evening out. "You don't have to do this, Leo. I know you have a hot date tonight."

"This is more important, Charlotte," Leo assured me. "You are my friend and you need help. I'm here until you can recite that book backwards and forwards. The date can wait."

I stared at the energy drink in my hand. This test felt hopeless, but Leo wasn't giving up on me. He never gave up on anyone, come to think of it. He wouldn't give up on me.

Leo stood up and walked around the table, putting his hands on my shoulders. It was a simple gesture. It wasn't romantic or sexy, yet it filled my heart. Even if Leo never felt the way I did about him, he still cared about me. He didn't have to stay here and help me study- he was choosing to. He was just that awesome of a guy. I loved him, even if I couldn't have him as my own. He was my friend, and if that's all that I could get, I would take it. Having Leo in my life as a friend was better than not having him.

Besides, he'd given up his date night to come help me. That had to count for something.

He squeezed my shoulders, making my heart ache for more. I knew that a shoulder squeeze was as much as I was ever going to get from him. "Okay, then. Let's start at the beginning..."

"And that concludes our auction. Thank you to all of our bidders and to Mr. Sebastian Belrose."

I leaned against the back wall and let out a huge sigh of relief. The auction was over. My work here was done. Everything was now in the hands of the auction house and Realtor, so I could go back to my normal job and not be doing double duty. For the first time in weeks, I was free. After the gala last night, and the auction all day today, I was beat. But, with everything finally finished, I could finally relax.

My sigh turned into a yawn, which I quickly stifled. I'd been up since before dawn making sure that everyone and everything was ready for the auction today. Luckily, the auction house run by Ava's aunt had their act together. Even my least favorite auctioneer in the world managed to show up on time and do a good job.

My stomach rumbled, reminding me that the last meal I ate was coffee and a granola bar sometime around sunrise. I needed to eat soon or I'd be chewing on the curtains. I was half surprised my stomach growls hadn't accidentally made bids during the auction they were so loud.

I turned and hurried down the hall to the kitchen. The warm, yellow space was quiet after the hustle and bustle of the auction floor. I grabbed a glass of milk along with some cheese and crackers left over from the gala the night before. I had hoped there would be leftover chicken, but everyone had eaten all of it.

Thinking of the gala made me think of Leo. Really, everything made me think of Leo, but pretending it was the gala made me feel a little less obsessed. I hadn't been able to talk to him all day, despite my best efforts. Either we were in too public a place or someone had been calling my name all day.

My hand rose to my lips, remembering the kiss. The way his lips pressed firm against mine. The heat and the desire. I needed to find him. I needed another kiss.

But only after I got a little bit of food in me.

I let out a happy little moan as I bit down on the cheese. It was good cheese, some sort of cheddar with a delicious saltiness, but hunger really was the best spice. It took all my willpower not to stuff the entire plate into my mouth.

"There you are," Bastian said, entering the kitchen. He watched as I stuffed another slice of cheese and cracker into my mouth and barely chewed it before swallowing. "We're done!"

"Thank heaven," I replied, stuffing another slice of cheese down my gullet. I was starving.

Bastian leaned against the counter, watching me for a moment before pushing the quickly emptying plate a little closer to me. "Will you do me a favor?"

"That's how you got me to help you with this auction..." I narrowed my eyes a little and paused. "What do you want?"

Bastian chuckled and grinned. "This one's easy. Can you arrange for Ava's father and his girlfriend to come to the island tomorrow?"

That was an easy request. Besides, I liked Ava's father. I grinned at him. "Sure. It shouldn't be a problem."

I looked down at the plate. The cheese was almost gone but I was still hungry. At least the raw edge of starvation was no longer gnawing on my belly, but I knew I needed to a real meal soon.

"You're the best," Bastian told me, coming around and giving me a big hug. He held me there for a moment longer than necessary. I wondered what he was contemplating when he asked, "Charlotte, you like Ava right?"

"Are you crazy?" I asked, giving him a little push. "I love her. You need to marry her, you know that, right?"

Surprise crossed his face and then happiness. He grinned widely before wrapping me up in a bone-breaking hug. "I'll get right on that," he promised.

"You better," I gasped, finally breaking free. I could see his brain already working on something, and I hoped it had something to do with Ava. And a ring.

If it didn't, this fairy god-mother was going to have to go to work again.

"You go shake people's hands," I told Bastian, waving him off with my hand. "I'll get the tickets set up for Mr. Fairchild."

He grinned one last time before heading out of the kitchen and back into the fray.

I looked down at the counter. All my cheese and crackers were gone, but I was still hungry. I sighed. I would have to figure out something for dinner soon, but first I needed to do my job.

I pulled out my phone and sent a quick email to Bastian's secretary about getting everything arranged. Private jet, limo pickup- the usual. Then a quick text to tell her to check her email. I grinned, knowing that I had Bastian's staff trained well. It certainly made my job a lot easier.

I put the cheese dish in the dishwasher and headed back to the auction room. The closer I got, the more crowded it became. I saw Bastian shaking hands with Jack while Emma clutched what looked like a small painting to her chest.

I turned, thinking I would check with the auction house one last time and ran smack dab into Leo's chest. His masculine strength and scent surrounded me as he chuckled. I put my hand on his chest in an attempt to steady myself, but just touching him made my head spin faster. I could feel the muscles of his chest through his dress shirt.

"Leo!" I gasped, still spinning on having him near. I loved the way his name felt in my mouth- it was almost like kissing him.

"Charlotte," he replied with a smile. Damn, that smile made my heart flutter. How did he make me feel so nervous? I'd known him for ten years, yet he still made my heart flutter and stomach flip like I was still thirteen staring up at the handsome college man.

"Hi," I murmured, not taking my hand off him.

"Congratulations on the successful auction," he said, looking around the auction. His hand covered mine, keeping it pressed to his chest. "I heard everything sold."

"The auction house will have the final numbers for me, but it looks like we surpassed our goals." I nodded, desperately trying to keep a professional face on since we were still very much in a public place. The heat of his hand was sending my thoughts skittering like marbles, though. "I saw you bid on several items. Thank you."

Leo shrugged like bidding on paintings worth hundreds

of thousands of dollars was nothing. "I liked them. And it all goes to a good cause. The money isn't just going to kids like Bastian. It's going to kids like you." His eyes focused on mine and dilated slightly. "I would help you a million times over."

Heat flushed in my cheeks and I bit my lip trying to keep myself from spiraling into giddiness. "Thank you, Leo," I whispered.

He leaned forward, his hand still pressing mine to his chest, until he could whisper in my ear. "What are you doing right now?"

"Right now?" I shivered with anticipation of having his lips so close. I wanted another kiss so badly. "I was going to go get something to eat and then open a bottle of wine and watch the sun set. Why?"

Please, please say you want to do that with me... I silently begged. *We can even skip the wine and the sunset...*

"Would you be interested in eating with me? I have reservations for two," he replied, his breath tickling my cheek.

"Yes," I replied immediately, my voice coming out squeaky and far too excited. One of the auction guests looked over weirdly at me and my fevered reply, but I didn't care. The butterflies in my stomach were doing a cheer routine over the fact that we were going to eat together. I cleared my throat, attempting to use my professional voice. "Yes, I would love that."

"Good," he said with a grin that lit up his eyes. "Go change into something comfortable, and meet me in the kitchen in ten minutes."

"Okay," I breathlessly responded. On impulse, I kissed his cheek before darting away to go change.

When I looked back, his hand was on his cheek and he was smiling.

Upstairs, I quickly put on a sundress and ran a brush through my hair. It felt good to be out of my work clothes and heels and in something light. I carefully put my glasses in their case on my nightstand. They were just for work and mostly to adjust for screen glare, but they seemed to make my intelligence more believable.

I glanced one last time at the mirror, making sure I looked ready. The mirror me grinned back, looking happier than I had in years. I let my dark hair stay loose around my shoulders, but put a rubber band around my wrist in case I needed it put up later. I couldn't believe the sparkle that Leo could put in my brown eyes.

Dinner with Leo meant kissing with Leo. Maybe more than kissing. I did a little happy dance around the room, glad that no one could see me. This was the kind of thing I had dreamed of for years.

With minutes to spare, I ran downstairs to the kitchen. I wondered if we were going to Adele's restaurant, or someplace else. Leo had said to dress comfortably, so I knew we couldn't be going anywhere fancy. The surprise of it was intoxicating.

Leo was waiting for me, standing by the kitchen door with a large picnic basket. He wore simple well-worn jean shorts and a clean white t-shirt that made the light blue of his eyes even more prominent. My middle turned to gooey mush at the sight of him.

"Ready?" he asked, grinning as I came forward. The late

afternoon sunlight was already brightening the kitchen and highlighting the golds in Leo's short hair.

I nodded, too much excitement welling up within me to speak. I was going on a date with Leo. A real date. Not an imaginary one, or a lunch meeting, or accidentally ending up at the same bar- a real, live date.

"Good," Leo said, holding out a hand for mine. He held onto the picnic basket with the other and together we stepped out into the hot Caribbean afternoon.

I was glad I had chosen a sundress. The sun beat down on my dark hair and had me wishing for the delicious air conditioned house again. Working inside had spoiled me. I hoped Leo had picked out a shady spot for us.

Leo guided me past the walkway down to the beach. I frowned slightly, but kept up. If we weren't having a picnic on the beach, I wasn't quite sure where we were going. He tugged gently, guiding me away from the house and over to the helicopter pad where one of the company helicopters was waiting.

"Where are we going, Leo?" I asked as he brought me over and helped me inside.

"It's a surprise," he answered with a naughty grin. "You'll like it."

I settled into the leather seats of the helicopter and put on my headset while the pilot began to power up the engine. Murdoch, Leo's bodyguard, was already seated in the co-pilot's seat looking scary and intimidating as usual. He turned as I settled and gave me a curt nod. I had no idea how old he was, just that he was as big as a mountain and strong as four men. His coal black eyes saw everything, but his stern expression implied he didn't like anything he saw. As far as bodyguards went, Murdoch was definitely the scariest one I had ever met.

Leo sat next to me, grabbing my hand as we started to lift into the air. My mouth was dry and my heart fluttered in my chest as we rose. I hoped he didn't notice that my hands were clammy with sweat. I'd been on helicopters dozens of times. It was one of the perks of working for billionaires that I never got caught in traffic to important meetings because that's how we always traveled. I'd even been on helicopters with Leo before, but this was different.

This was a *date*.

12

———

The thrum of the engines vibrated the entire helicopter. I loved the feeling flying in a helicopter gave me. It was so easy and free. In a helicopter, I could go anywhere. There were no limits to how high or how fast. I wasn't human anymore, in here, I was a dragonfly.

Leo squeezed my hand. From the light in his eyes, he was a dragonfly too. There wasn't anyone else that I wanted to be a dragonfly with more.

The copter skimmed the shore for a while, each wave merging into the next as we sped onward. Dark shapes moved in the water, leviathans of the deep. But we flew past them without a care. Onward, into the island the helicopter flew.

The only flights I'd been on around the island were just ones for coming and going from the mainland. I'd never really had the chance to explore the island, especially this past trip. I'd been so busy working the auction that I'd barely even had time to leave the mansion, let alone explore.

The helicopter flew toward the middle of the island. Key

Island was the playground of the rich and famous. Billion-aires, movie stars, CEO's, and rock stars all came to stay on this island. The edges of the coast were lined with beach front homes and white sandy beaches.

However, the interior of the island was different. The locals lived more inland, and the further from the beaches we went, the more the tropical jungle took hold. I'd never had a reason to go to the center of the island, but that was where it looked like the helicopter was taking us. I wondered just what Leo had planned for us. This was far more than just a simple picnic.

I peered out at the lush greenery and steep mountains that made up the center of the island. As we came around a cliff, a beautiful waterfall emerged. It was huge and picture perfect. I looked over at Leo and he grinned, nodding back to the window.

The pilot took the helicopter to the base of the waterfall and then rose up alongside it. The water rushing past combined with the heady sensation of rising made me dizzy. Leo laughed as I shook my head to clear the vertigo, and then told the pilot to land.

The pilot took the helicopter up as high as possible, letting us see the whole island spread out before us like a map. The green of the forests gave way to a white ring that led to pale blue waters that turned dark as they reached for the horizon. It was absolutely breathtaking.

Slowly, the pilot brought us down to a small field just a stone's throw from the rushing waterfall. We landed with a soft thud, and Leo took off his headset and opened the door. He grabbed the picnic basket and jumped out, turning to offer me his hand once he landed. I reached for him, trying to stay graceful even though my movements were clumsy with excitement.

Leo helped me out, holding me close as the helicopter blades whirred above our heads. The wind of the blades whipped my hair into my eyes and plastered my dress to my legs as the pilot rose once more into the air.

"Is Murdoch not coming?" I asked Leo, noticing that his ever-present shadow hadn't gotten off the helicopter. The two of us were very much alone.

"This place is only accessible by helicopter," Leo explained, taking my hand and leading me away from our landing spot. "Murdoch felt it was safe enough, but they'll come back and get us whenever I call."

I watched as the helicopter rose and dipped, disappearing behind the crags of the mountain holding the waterfall. It was so quiet now that I could hear the gentle roar of the waterfall in the distance. It took me a moment, but I realized that I was finally alone with Leo. I was glad we weren't on the beach or out at a restaurant, because then I would have to share him with the crowd. Here, we were in our own secret little world where no one could interrupt or bother us.

I turned to find him opening the picnic basket and spreading out a blanket. From where he was, we would have the perfect view of the waterfall without the sound of water drowning out our words.

"I've never been here before," I said, picking at a blade of long grass and listening to the serenity of nature. The sound of the water filled was in the background, birds sung out, and the gentle hum of a bumblebee surrounded me. It was incredibly peaceful, especially after the hustle and bustle of the auction. It was exactly what I needed.

"I found it by accident," Leo explained. "I don't think even the locals know about this place."

"It's beautiful." I looked up at him and he smiled. He was beautiful.

"Would you like to see the falls?" Leo offered, pausing in setting out dinner. "They're kind of the reason I brought you here. I thought you'd like them."

"Yes!" I eagerly agreed. I was so glad I had eaten the cheese and crackers. I wanted to see the falls, especially with sunset coming soon. I could only imagine the rainbows that would form as the light hit the splashing water. Besides, I wasn't so hungry I couldn't wait anymore. If Leo wanted to show them to me, then I wanted to see them.

Leo laughed at my enthusiasm and took my hand. We followed the meadow to the edge of the water. The sound of water filled my ears. The waterfall plummeted from a hundred feet up, crashing into a pond of blue water that sparkled and shimmered in the sun. It looked like something out of a fairy tale it was so perfect.

The roar and power of the water was intense and breathtaking. I knew I could stare at it all day and never grow tired of watching the water dance and fly from the cliffs. I wished I could soar along with it, flying like a bird down its silver beauty and drown without dying in the depths of the pond. I imagined it would feel like falling in love.

"This is so beautiful," I whispered, thinking the roar of the water would drown out my words.

"Yes, it is," Leo agreed, somehow having heard me. I turned to see he wasn't looking at the waterfall. He was looking at me.

I'd waited all day to have some alone time with Leo, and now we were together in front of the most beautiful waterfall I'd ever seen. Spray from the falling water misted our clothes and hair, forming dew drops that sparkled like tiny worlds of wonder.

"Leo," I whispered. His name barely left my lips when he kissed me. The world spun too fast and gravity no longer worked, but I didn't care. One kiss had been enough to show me that Leo was interested. This kiss blew that kiss out of the water.

This was a waterfall kiss.

His lips were firm and confident, his tongue tasting and caressing like he couldn't get enough of my taste. I moaned softly, whimpering at his sensual touch that was driving me wild. I'd never been kissed like this before.

Finally, I was getting to kiss Leo. My Leo, the man I had loved for years. And here was the proof that he cared for me right back. My hand caressed his jaw, feeling the end of day stubble that rasped against my lips. I loved how masculine and strong he was.

Slowly, gasping for breath, we both pulled back.

Leo grinned, the corners of his mouth twisting into a beautiful smile. "Wow."

I kissed him again, feeling the same rush of want that threatened to overwhelm me. I couldn't get enough of him. I'd waited for so long, that now I couldn't wait any longer.

"Slow down, Speedy," Leo teased. "We have all night. Want to get closer to the waterfall?"

He was right. At this rate, I'd have the whole night finished in just a couple of minutes. I didn't need to rush things. We had time. I looked at the rushing water and nodded. The pool was crystal clear and made for the two of us to be alone in. "As long as you're with me."

I kicked off my shoes and stepped into the pool. The water was cold, but it felt good against the Caribbean heat. Leo was right beside me, holding my hand tightly in his.

I waded out, holding my dress up to keep it out of the water.

"Why don't you just take it off?" he asked, managing to keep a straight face.

I hesitated. I only had a pair of undies on underneath the dress. Thong undies.

Was I ready for that?

It took me all of two seconds to decide that yes, yes I was ready for that. I'd been ready to be naked with Leo for ten freaking years. But I didn't want to be the only one getting naked.

"Only if you do, too," I replied, slowly inching the skirt of the dress up. Leo's eyes went to my bare thigh, the blue slowly disappearing to the dilating black of his pupils.

"Done," he said, whipping his shirt over his head and tossing it to the shore.

I nearly dropped my dress hem. His chest gleamed in the sun, muscled and perfect. He liked to keep active, but he usually stayed dressed around the office, so I didn't get a regular look at his body.

He smirked as he caught me looking. "Were you going to take it off or what?" he teased, loosening the zipper on his shorts. My breath caught a little. It was time. I closed my eyes and took a deep breath, hoping that I looked as good to him as he did to me.

I pulled the dress up and over my head, balling it up and tossing it onto the pebbly beach. I stared at the water for a moment before raising my eyes to look at Leo. Part of me was terrified that he'd back out, suddenly remembering that I was Bastian's little sister and he shouldn't be looking at me like that.

But he didn't. He stared and the reaction in his boxers told me that he didn't think of me as anyone's little sister. Without looking, he tossed his shorts behind him, narrowly missing dropping them in the water.

I hugged my arms around me as he came closer. I stood mid thigh deep in the water. He looked me up and down, desire and admiration filling his face. I bit my lip a little, still nervous as to what he was going to say next.

"Wow," he whispered, stopping in front of me. "Just wow."

"Thanks," I giggled, suddenly giddy and ridiculously happy. "You look pretty 'wow' yourself."

"You'd know," he teased. "The first time I met you, I was naked."

"I remember," I replied, my voice suddenly going husky. I took a step forward. "But you looked more like this-"

And then I pulled down his boxers, soaking them in the water.

"Not fair," Leo growled, pulling me into him. He was already hard and erect and pushing against the small triangle of cloth that pretended to be my underwear.

The water around our knees was cold, but the heat searing through me at Leo's nearness was enough to set it to boiling. He kicked at his drenched boxers, reaching down and tossing them to dry on the shore while still pulling me into him. His hands tightened on my hips and I couldn't stop myself from rocking into the pleasure his thick heat. Every fiber of my being ached to have this. I wanted it now, yet I wanted it to last forever.

"I don't remember this part," I said, pressing my chest into his muscled one and trying to maintain my playful demeanor. "Even though it's what I've wanted for a long time."

He laughed, a low, sexy sound that turned my nipples hard and made me ache deep in my core.

"You want this?" He rocked his hips against mine. He grinned like the cocky, confident, alpha, billionaire, jerk I knew he had inside of him. I wanted that part of him too. I wanted all of him.

I couldn't help it, but my pulse fluttered and my skin flushed. I wanted him. Bad. I nodded, unable to speak.

He lowered his head to put his perfect lips to my shoulder, pressing his mouth to my skin and sending a shiver of pure desire rocketing through me. I couldn't help the moan or the arch of my hips to his.

His fingers traced the tiny black string still plastered to my hips as he grinned and met my eyes. I was instantly lost in their blue depths, lost to their swirling lust and power. My breath caught in my chest and I couldn't move. I was paralyzed with want.

I barely felt the way his fingers hooked on the string and pulled. I didn't think as I kicked my legs free of the black triangle of fabric and tossed it to the side to stand completely naked, pressed to Leo like I had always wanted. The world was spinning too fast and blood was rushing in my ears. I was finally with Leo.

The corner of his mouth tipped up higher, cocky as hell in his knowledge of what was going to happen next. Me, on the other hand was a trembling leaf of desire. I wanted this more than I wanted to breathe, yet I couldn't begin to believe it was real. This was too good to be a dream. It was everything I'd ever wanted.

I bit my lip, unsure of what to do next. I wanted to impale myself on him and kiss him and taste him and touch him and have him touch me all at once. Years of sexual fantasies were all bubbling to the surface all at once and I didn't know which one I wanted first.

Leo took control, bringing his hand to my chin and cupping it with his fingers. He brought my lips to his, demanding a kiss that made me forget everything. The kiss grew hotter and more intense with every second. Lips and tongues collided as our bodies pressed together.

His lips ventured from mine, kissing and caressing down the side of my neck until he found the super-sensitive spot just under my jaw and ear. The rough stubble of his chin scraped at my skin in the most tantalizing way, making me moan and writhe for more. Yet, the only thing I could do was to let my head fall back and drink in ever exquisite sensation of his mouth on my skin. I wanted more. So much more.

Putting a hand on my hip, he guided my body without me realizing it until my back was pressed against his chest. His manhood pressed hot and hard to my ass while his hands went to my breasts, his mouth still on my shoulders. I gasped as he rolled one nipple between his thumb and fore-finger. White hot electricity threaded it's way from his fingers, down my spine to pool in between my thighs.

"Leo," I gasped, arching my back into his chest and loving that he didn't move. The hand on my hip splayed out across my stomach, pulling my body closer to his. He was so warm against the spray of the water that I pushed closer, wanting his heat everywhere. Slowly, his hand slipped south.

The heat settling in my lower stomach was a living thing now. Leo's fingers slid down, brushing past my pleasure center so smoothly that I shivered against him as he slowly found his way to me. My legs spread automatically to give him access.

My eyes closed as his fingers found their rhythm. He held me to him, using my breathing as a guide for what pleasure he was causing. Two fingers swirled and I focused on the glowing orb of light forming in my groin that was going to explode into white ecstasy at any moment. I could feel the beat of his heart through his cock pressing firmly into my ass.

He wanted me.

I closed my eyes as the sensations swirled and coalesced into a burning sun that overtook me completely. Leo's name fell from my lips, more wordless cry than name as my world shuddered to pleasure. I'd had orgasms before, but never like this. Never this powerful or all-consuming. The only thing that was different was Leo. My knees gave out, yet I didn't fall. Water splashed around us, yet I wasn't cold.

Leo held me. He kept me held close to him even as I went limp from his touches.

Possessive. That was the only way to describe the way he held me.

Slowly, I regained my strength to stand, even though my head was still buzzing with the aftershocks of Leo's fingers. My tongue was too thick to speak and I was light-headed with lack of blood to my brain. It was fantastic.

If he could give that level of orgasm to me, that quickly, with just a touch of his hand, the thought of what he could do to me with the rest of him had me panting. With a core full of burning desire, I turned to face him.

I nearly came again at the intensity of his expression. Lust had his pupils dilated to almost blackness and I couldn't look away. It was the way I had always wanted him to look at me. He had only ever looked at me like this in my dreams. To see it in reality was a thousand times better than any fantasy.

I lifted my leg, hooking it around his waist and drawing him even closer. The heat of his manhood seared against my exposed skin and I ached with desperate need. I could feel the muscles of his ass and lower back contract as he rocked into me.

He looked back to shore, a twist of pain on his face.

"What?" I asked, suddenly afraid he was going to change his mind. We were so close to fulfilling all my fantasies that I held onto him as hard as I could.

"There's a condom in my shorts." He grimaced. "But they're way over there."

I followed his gaze to the shore. It wasn't far, but the idea of him leaving my embrace, even for a millisecond was unbearable. I put my palm to his cheek.

"It's okay. I'm on the pill."

He frowned, but his erection throbbed against my entrance. "You sure?"

I nodded, peering into his eyes. "Yes. I trust you. I always have."

Our eyes locked. No one had ever looked at me like this. Dangerous heat and desire flooded his gaze as he slid into me, completing me in a way I never thought possible. His body was made to fit mine. Every muscle in my body tightened, wanting to take more and more of him inside of me. I was afraid to breathe, afraid that somehow oxygen would take up space that Leo could fill.

"Leo..." I whispered, losing myself to the pleasure only he could give me.

He thrust upward, filling me to the hilt. I cried out with unbridled lust. I wanted more. Needed more. My leg tightened around his hips, begging him to keep filling me. The muscles of his back and hips were drawn tight, bulging and working with every thrust. My nails found purchase on his skin, hard enough to leave a thin red line but not to break the skin. I had an urge to mark him as mine.

My belly tightened, the glowing ball of pleasure suddenly exploding within me. My breasts arched into his chest, feeling his heat consume me as I lost myself once again to his pleasure. The ease of the orgasm was almost frightening. With Leo, I barely had to concentrate, barely had to try to find the mountain of pleasure that other men had to scale for hours.

"Fuck, Charlotte," he gasped, each syllable more ragged than the last. The raw need in his voice was a testament to how greatly his need matched mine.

The water behind us thundered with power. Spray drifted up in mist that caught on the tips of Leo's dark hair and eyelashes, making him look more dreamlike than ever. I could hardly believe this was real. He was here. With me. Every fantasy, every dream I'd ever had of him paled in reality. Years of desires burnt and flamed within me, finding that the reality of Leo was far better than anything I ever could have imagined.

His hands gripped my hips and ass, holding to me as he thrusted and filled me. Yet his eyes were always on mine. Full of love and lust and everything I had ever wanted.

"Leo, come for me..." I gasped. I wasn't sure if he heard me over the roar of the falls, but I needed him. I was half afraid that I would wake up at any moment and find that this was just a dream. That his strong arms holding me, his heat against the cold water around our legs, and the intensity of his gaze would be nothing but a vivid fantasy.

"Mine." His word was strong and deep. My chest pounded with anticipation as his rhythm built to climax. The intensity of his eyes made it hard to breathe and I couldn't focus on anything but the immense pleasure he was giving me. Heat and pleasure coiled in my belly again, threatening yet a third release in less time than it usually took me to get one.

His eyes claimed me, his gaze holding me captive as we reached the threshold of tolerable pleasure together. I nodded, silently begging for him to release. The knowledge of him falling into me was already pushing me over the tipping point. But I wanted to fall with him.

Contractions rippled through his back and his strong arms pulled me deeper into him as he delved for the last time into my body.

"Charlotte!" My name was a benediction from his lips as he lost himself within me. My inner muscles pulled and clenched at his thick shaft as I lost myself to the most powerful orgasm yet. I had no idea how he could melt me like this. It was beyond anything I'd ever experienced.

Yet I wasn't surprised by it.

Leo's body stilled beneath me, his breath coming in ragged gasps that made me ache for more.

"Every fantasy," he gasped. "Every single one was nothing compared to that."

I grinned and nodded. He was right.

It was every single one come true all at once.

13

———

"You're shivering," Leo said, wrapping his arms around me. "Let's get you back where it's warm."

I nodded, my teeth chattering so hard I was afraid I might break them. Up until about three minutes ago, I hadn't noticed how cold the water was or that the sun was setting. I had been too hot and bothered to notice anything but Leo. Now, I was freezing.

With Leo's arm around me, we picked up our clothing. He frowned at his soaked boxers, but carried them up as we hurried out from the shade of the waterfall back to the meadow with the waiting picnic basket. Shivering, I pulled my dress over my head and spread out on the blanket, soaking up the hot sun. Leo set his wet clothes on the grass to dry, going commando in his shorts.

The sun was setting over the horizon, but away from the spray of the waterfall it was warm to the point of being hot. I stopped shivering fairly quickly and as soon as I was warm, my stomach started to rumble.

"Dinner?" Leo asked, opening up the basket and pulling

things out. The smells already emanating from the basket had my mouth watering. I was hungry from all the exercise we just did.

I sat up and nodded. "Yes, please."

There was fried chicken, mashed potatoes, fresh pineapple slices, and fluffy white biscuits with butter already melted inside of them. It was a feast. He grinned handing me a plate and spreading the rest of the food out on the blanket before me so I could eat more at my leisure.

As I took a bite of the biscuit, I didn't care that I was supposed to be watching what I ate. If the response I just got from Leo was any indication, I didn't need to worry too much about how I looked. I really only cared what one person thought of my body, and the fact that he now was sitting next to me with his hand creeping up my thigh told me that he liked what he saw.

The sharp edge of hunger dulled, and I slowed down on the meal enough to taste it. I let out a happy sigh, looking over at the man who had just made all my daydreams come true. I pinched myself, just to make sure that it was real, glad that the little red welt on my arm hurt.

"Don't pinch too hard," Leo said, noting what I was doing. "I don't want to wake up either."

"This is just how I imagined it," I said softly, looking around at the beauty surrounding us. Everything was perfect.

Leo took another bite of food. "Me too," he confessed.

"I can't believe we didn't do this sooner." I closed my eyes and taking in a deep breath of the humid Caribbean air. The unspoken question of *"Why didn't we?"* hung in the air.

I opened my eyes to find Leo staring at me. He dropped

his eyes and evaluated the biscuit in his hands. He swallowed hard.

"I didn't think I deserved you," he said after a moment, his voice low. "I still don't."

I set the last of my meal down, leaning forward and putting my palm on his cheek. "You do deserve me," I informed him.

"You are everything I could want, Charlotte." His eyes met mine. "Everything. I shouldn't have everything. No matter how much I want it."

"What about what I want?" I asked, a little angry that he had put me on a pedestal for so long. I didn't want to be on a pedestal. I wanted to be with him. "I've known you for ten years and you're the only one that I want."

He sighed, his blue eyes holding back something. Tension crept into his shoulders. He plucked a blade of grass, twirling it between his fingers before crushing it and tossing it to the side. "I still have secrets. Things you don't know about. Things that would make you change your mind about me."

"Like what?" I tossed a crumb from my biscuit at him. It bounced off his eyebrow and he glared at me.

I didn't believe he could have any deep dark secrets. Besides, short of him telling me he was an ax murderer, there wasn't anything he could say that would change how I felt about him.

Leo's eyes darkened and he looked away. Indecision filled his expression so strongly I could feel it eating away at my stomach. He sighed, ripping another blade of grass from the earth.

"Tell me, Leo," I said softly, pulling gently on his chin to face me again. "Nothing you say can change the way I feel about you. You should know that by now."

The corner of his mouth twitched up in a small smile, but it didn't touch his eyes. He took a deep breath. "I used to have a gambling problem. A big one."

"Gambling? That's it?" I repeated. That was definitely not ax murderer, but he felt it was a big deal so I wasn't going to dismiss it. I softened my voice. "Like betting on horses or poker kind of gambling?"

"Yes, both." His voice was wooden and he looked out past me. "If you could bet money on it, I did it. Football games were my specialty."

"Were you any good at it?" I asked, thinking of how terrible my luck was at a casino.

"Very."

I nodded slowly. The idea of gambling contrasted with the Leo I knew. Leo was always in control, always throwing out some sort of joke or causing trouble. I had difficulty seeing him in a situation where he couldn't be guaranteed to win. I supposed that's where the thrill to him came. He was the type of person who always won, and gambling didn't allow for that.

"I just realized that I've never seen you bet on anything. Not even a five dollar bet with Bastian or Gabe or even the office basketball tournament pool. You must be very committed to it," I said. I had to wonder what else I had missed about him. "What made you stop?"

"I nearly lost everything." The lines of his face hardened and he finally brought his gaze back to mine. "So I stopped and I don't gamble any more."

"And you thought I would hate you because of that?"

"It's not something I'm proud of." Leo's eyes begged for forgiveness from me. "It's an addiction. One I fight every day. It's not exactly a lovable trait."

I leaned forward and kissed his lips. He didn't pull away, but he didn't kiss me back.

"I still like you. A lot. Maybe even more than like." I grinned hoping he would smile at my words.

Leo looked up and I loved the joyful surprise that filled his face. He kissed my forehead. "See, this is why I really don't deserve you. I tell you a secret that would send most girls running to the hills and you smile and make it all seem okay."

I rolled my eyes. "You keep up with that and I'm going to have to do something about it. You deserve me. End of story."

"If you say so," he replied, shrugging off his previous unease.

I laughed as he moved behind me so I sat between his legs. He wrapped his arms around my shoulders and I leaned back, loving the warm heat of his chest pressing into my back. The sun hung low on the horizon, turning into a red ball in the sky and casting dark orange shadows across the field. Soon the stars would come out overhead and already the frogs and crickets were starting their nocturnal songs. Leo hugged me tight. "Okay, your turn to tell me a secret."

"What?" I sat up and looked at him. "I never agreed to that."

He raised his eyebrows and grinned, knowing full well that I hadn't, but wanting my secrets anyway. I sighed. Leo always got what he wanted.

"I have had a crush on you since the day we met," I admitted.

"Charlotte, I'm pretty sure that the aliens on Mars know that," Leo replied, rolling his eyes.

"You knew?" I felt a blush sear across my face.

"You blush every time you look at me," Leo informed me. "Just like you're blushing now."

I buried my face in my hands, trying to hide the evidence. "That just makes it worse. You *knew*. All along."

"It was cute," he said, kissing my hair.

"That's terrible," I groaned. My crush had known all along. To be honest, I hadn't been very subtle about it, but that didn't make the shame of being found out any less.

"It made it that much harder to say no to you," Leo explained, running his hand down my hair. "I knew I shouldn't feel the way I do about you, but you were just so damn perfect and sweet."

"Yeah, like a kid sister," I mumbled. "Did you even like me back? Or is all of this-" I indicated to the two of us "-a new emotion for you?"

"Not new. I've liked you for years, but I had to keep my distance or your brother would give me two black eyes and a broken spleen." Leo chuckled. "But now, I think I can take him in a fight, especially if he's busy with his new girlfriend."

I giggled. "So, you did like me? Even though I was Bastian's scrawny little kid sister?"

"At first you were Bastian's scrawny kid sister," Leo admitted. "But when you walked into our office during your freshman year of college, you weren't scrawny anymore. You were this transformed, beautiful woman. And there was all this spunk and energy to you that I couldn't stay away from. Why do you think I always brought you coffee to our meetings?"

"I just thought you liked coffee and were flirting with the baristas," I admitted.

"Well, maybe a couple of flirtations, but you were the one I liked." Leo chuckled, the vibrations of his laughter reverberating through his chest and into my back. "But, the coffee was my way of telling you that I cared without having Bastian beat me up for hitting on his kid sister."

"So what changed?" I asked. "I mean, I noticed you've put on some muscle lately, but..."

Leo hugged me hard, stopping my words and making me giggle. "What changed? I saw how happy Mr. Grump-face Bastian was and I wanted to feel that too."

"Those two certainly are something special," I agreed. I thought of how Ava smiled at Bastian and I knew that I had that same smile for Leo. I always had it, but now, it wasn't just me smiling. Now Leo was smiling with me.

Leo let out a slow, long breath. "It's more than that, actually. I'm greedy, and weak, and I wanted that. I couldn't see a good reason to deny myself anymore." He paused for a moment. "I'd feel guilty, except you feel so good in my arms that I can't."

"You're not greedy or weak," I said. Leo was many things, but both of those words were the last things I would ever call him. I snuggled back into him and he hugged me close to him. The sun was almost gone now, but the dark was inviting and warm here.

"Tell me a real secret." Leo's voice was low as darkness spread over us like a blanket.

I took a deep breath. He had told me a secret, it really was only fair that I did to.

"Only Bastian knows this," I said slowly, pressing my hands into my thighs. My palms were suddenly coated with sweat. This wasn't something I wanted Leo to know about me, but something I thought he should. Lovers should know their history. "He only knows because he helped me deal with all the paperwork."

"You don't have to tell me, Charlotte," Leo said, picking up on my distress. "Pick something else."

"No," I said, shaking my head. "You should know what you've gotten yourself into."

I paused. This was my secret. The one I hid from the world and even from myself. But, love was about sharing secrets and not being afraid of them. Love can't thrive where there is secrets.

"My parents died in a drug deal gone bad. I loved them because they were my parents, but after they died, I found out that they weren't good people." The words tumbled out in a rush. There was so much darkness in my past, so much that I didn't want to say.

"I'm sorry, Charlotte," Leo said quietly. I loved that he pulled me closer to him, sharing his strength with me and silently telling me he wasn't going to let me go.

I clung to him, praying that he wouldn't let go. "When I say they were drug dealers, I don't mean that they sold some brownies with special butter. They ruined people's lives. They were suspected of several murders."

I hoped that Leo didn't think I was like them. Their blood ran through my veins. They'd raised me until I was six and I was sure that a part of them was still with me. I had done my best to root out any bad habits they might have passed on, but there was no fighting genetics.

They were bad people. What made me any different than them?

What made me good enough for Leo? If either of us didn't deserve one another, I didn't deserve him.

Yet, Leo wasn't letting me go. If anything he was holding me tighter.

"I hate that they left me that secret. I hate that they left me." My voice faltered. "I still have nightmares about the day they died. Even though they weren't good people, they were all I had."

I pushed away the memory of leaving my home and everything I knew. How alone in the world I had felt and how terrified I was that no one would ever love me again. I was the orphaned daughter of drug dealers- who would want me?

I took a deep breath. "But, I'm glad I got Bastian instead of them," I informed him, putting strength back into my voice. That was the only part of my life that I was grateful to my parents for. They gave me the opportunity to have a brother like Bastian. "So, when you say that you don't deserve me, I don't believe it."

"I still think you're everything I could ever want." He pressed a kiss to the back of my head, his arms still tight around me. Never once during my confession did he loosen his hug.

I shifted my weight to look at him. Night was falling quickly and it wouldn't be long before I could no longer see his eyes, but for now, they were still blue. And full of love. "You've always been there for me and Bastian. If anything, I don't deserve you."

Leo brushed a strand of hair away from my eyes and held me tighter. "Now, it's my secret too. You don't have to carry it by yourself anymore."

He kissed my hair, holding me as close to him as possible, and for the first time in years, I felt truly wanted and safe.

THE HELICOPTER BLADES sliced through the air and hummed with power, but I barely noticed as it landed. Sleep tugged at my eyes and I couldn't resist it. I didn't mean to fall asleep in Leo's arms, but safe under his care with a blanket of stars, I had drifted off.

"Is it time to go?" I murmured, sleep blurring my voice.

"Shh," Leo whispered, picking me up and carrying me to the helicopter in his arms. Out of the corner of my eye I saw the black shadow of Murdoch leap down and scurry behind us to pick up our things.

I was nearly asleep again by the time the helicopter took off. I couldn't believe how tired I was, but given that I had been up since before dawn, ran an auction, had amazing sex under a waterfall, and finally got to tell Leo my darkest secrets, I supposed I was allowed to be a little sleepy.

Leo took my hand as the helicopter soared through the air back to the mansion. His hand was warm and strong around mine and I knew that he'd never let me go. He knew my secret now and he didn't care. He didn't care what my parents had done, just that I was his.

It made me love him even more.

I didn't remember the flight home at all, but the jolt of the helicopter landing startled me awake. With blurry eyes and clumsy feet, I jumped out of the chopper. Leo helped me away from the whirling blades. I held onto him, trusting that he would make sure I didn't hurt myself.

"Come on, sleepy head," Leo said gently, scooping me up in his arms once we cleared the helicopter pad. "You can't even walk you're so tired."

I didn't fight him, even though I usually hated being carried. Being carried usually made me feel small and helpless, but not with Leo. With his arms around me, I was precious and protected. I snuggled into his shoulder, breathing in his comforting scent and letting him be in control.

I feel him take the stairs, his strong arms and back lifting me effortlessly. It was only at the top that he let out a chuckle and shifted my weight around. To be fair, they were steep stairs and I had a stomach full of chicken.

"Here you go, sleeping beauty." Leo carefully laid me down on the bed and then pulled off my sandals. He paused, but left the dress on since it was now dry and moving me would be more work than it was worth.

"Don't leave," I begged, catching his hand before he could turn. "Stay with me."

He paused, clearly thinking about my brother sleeping just a few rooms down. "Okay," he whispered, kicking off his own shoes and pulling off his t-shirt before sliding into bed next to me.

Now that he was with me, I pulled the dress up and over my head, pressing my bare skin against his. He wrapped his arms around me, placing my head on the hollow of his shoulder. He was so warm and comfortable, I knew I would never be content with a regular pillow ever again.

Leo's heart beat steadily in my ear, singing me back to sleep with every beat.

I slept, and for the first time in my life, the nightmares never came.

14

—————

I woke up sticky and hot with the sun in my eyes. But Leo was still in my bed. He was splayed out across the bed, snoring softly and taking up most of the room. I didn't care. He was here.

Sunlight filtered through the window, highlighting the soft golds and reds in his brown hair. His chest rose and fell, rhythmic and smooth and full of muscles and tanned skin. I couldn't believe how beautiful he was. Handsome was a word for men, but he was so much more than that. He was perfect, and even better, he was mine.

I was a lucky girl.

"Are you watching me sleep?" Leo's eyes stayed closed.

"Maybe." I grinned at him, even though he couldn't see me.

"That's kind of creepy," he informed me, keeping his eyes closed.

"But in a sweet, lovable kind of way, right?"

He opened one eye and one corner of his mouth tipped upward. "Definitely a sweet, lovable kind of way."

This was heaven. It had to be. There was no way that a person could feel this much joy and pleasure and not be dead. It just wasn't possible.

"Want to shower?" Leo asked, his voice low and deep as he rolled over and stretched.

"Yes, please." I nodded. I was covered in sweat and sex from yesterday, and besides, Leo hadn't seen my shower yet.

I had picked this room in the mansion as my bedroom for a reason. The view of the ocean was excellent, but certainly not the best in the building. I had chosen this room for the attached bathroom. The bathroom made it the best room in the house.

First off, the bathroom was about as big as a bedroom. There was the small toilet room off to the side and his and her sinks. The over-sized tub overlooking the ocean was certainly a selling point to the awesomeness of the bathroom, and despite having enjoyed several baths in it, was still not the best part of the room. The shower, far and away, was.

The shower was big enough for four people, with eight shower heads, a digital water thermometer which allowed different temperatures for the different heads, a rain feature, as well as a steam function and music selection. It was the best shower I had ever seen, and I worked for billionaires. I'd seen a lot of cool showers.

"Wow," Leo said, standing back and taking in the massive shower. "Do I need a college degree to operate it?"

I gave him a gentle push out of the way as I went to the sink and ran a brush through my hair before starting the water. "Just push preset number one," I told him.

Leo gave me a skeptical look before stepping inside the magic glass doors and pressing the button. The shower came to life with all eight jets and the rain feature all starting at the perfect temperature.

"I am never leaving your shower," Leo informed me, closing his eyes and enjoying the luxury of the spray. I watched him for a moment, loving the way the water sluiced down his muscles and how his skin gleamed when it was wet.

"I'm actually, really, really alright with that," I said, opening the shower door and joining him in the steamy water.

"I really like the way you look when you're wet," he said, his eyes going up and down my body.

I raised an eyebrow at him, knowing he meant with water but enjoying the double meaning. "You are so dirty. Will you hand me the shampoo?"

"Then you better get me clean," he teased, handing me the shampoo.

I quickly opened the bottle and poured some in my hair. I loved the way my shampoo smelled- floral but not girly.

"So this is how you always smell so damn good," Leo murmured, coming up behind me. The bare skin of his chest, legs, and groin pressing into my back. I leaned back slightly as he put his hands in my hair and started to massage my head with his fingers.

I moaned softly, feeling any remaining stress I could possibly have leave my body. It felt so good just to be touched and taken care of. I was usually the one taking care of everyone and everything that it felt amazing to be pampered.

"Lean your head back," Leo coaxed, pulling my hair into the water and rinsing the suds out. He carefully cupped his hand over my head to keep any of the bubbles from straying into my eyes. "Conditioner?"

I pointed to the corner where he had found the shampoo, unable to form sentences. Leo chuckled and added the creamy conditioner to my hair. I closed my eyes in bliss as he worked it into every strand, taking his time and making sure he did a thorough job.

"What do you have planned for the day?" he asked.

"Nothing," I moaned. He tipped my head under the spray of water again and started rinsing. "Well, once I send out a few emails and make sure the world isn't going to burn, nothing. After the gala and auction- I'm taking a day off."

"Good, you deserve a day off." He squeezed the water out of my hair and I sighed, sad that it was done.

"What do you have planned?" I asked, putting the shampoo bottle back in its holder.

"I was hoping to hang out with my girlfriend." He grinned at me.

I froze for a moment, my heart skittering and hoping. "Am I your girlfriend?" All my teenage dreams depended on his answer.

"Would you like to be?" Leo flashed me his confident, bad boy billionaire smile that made all this business deals fall into place.

I nodded, afraid my voice would come out as a high-pitched adolescent squeak.

Leo chuckled, pulling me to him and kissing me. I closed my eyes, soaking up the moment. Spray from the shower reminded me of our waterfall kiss from the day before and my body heated in response.

"All the other girls are going to be so jealous," I said once he released me from his kiss.

"They should be," he replied with a cocky grin.

I laughed, letting the sound echo around the shower for a moment. "What do you want to do today, *boyfriend*?"

I felt a little silly calling anyone *boyfriend*, especially Leo. He was most certainly not a boy and he was so much more than a friend to me.

"I was thinking of taking the boat out to a little beach I know. Thought maybe my girlfriend would like to come," he replied with a smile. "Why do you think I haven't pinned you up against that shower wall and had my way with you already? I'm saving up for something special."

A tremor of expected pleasure rippled through me. My legs parted slightly, wanting him to do just that. The idea of him taking me here, in the shower with all the water cascading around us... it made me wet with desire.

"I don't know if I can wait," I told him. My body was already warming to the idea.

He shook his head, taking a step forward and pressing his body to mine. He was hard and erect between my legs. Just a thrust of his hips and he would have me.

I pushed my back toward him and at the same time, he slipped his arms around my stomach, breathing in through his teeth.

"Charlotte," he whispered on his exhale. "You know that I can't resist you when you're like this."

A smirk crossed my face as I looked over my shoulder at him. I then began to move my hips forward and back slightly, teasing him by sliding myself against the top of his shaft. Leo let out a soft groan as his powerful hands moved up my sides, pulling me closer to him. My back was pressed against his muscular torso and I could feel the cadence of his breathing as our bodies pressed against each other.

"Is that turning you on?" I asked, despite already knowing the answer.

Leo leaned forward, bringing his lips to the side of my neck. He kissed the sensitive skin, sending a pleasurable tingle through my body.

"Did you really just ask me that?" he asked, playfully.

His hands moved upward a bit further and he cupped my breasts, squeezing them gently and sending a burst of pleasure into my body. His touch made me want him even more and I found myself pushing back against him a little harder.

"Just do it," I whispered, flirtatiously. "Be bad with me. Right now."

The pace of Leo's breathing began to increase as his hands moved across my front, touching all the right spots and causing me to get turned on even more. My entire body began to crave him. And even though we had just had sex the night before, I found myself wanting him more than ever.

"Please," I begged.

Leo exhaled, his breath hitting my shoulder. Then he lifted one of his hands from my breasts and brought it around to my upper back. His fingers slid along my skin and up my neck, until he reached my hairline. I bit my lower lip and gently closed my eyes, enjoying his touch. The way he handled me made me feel so wanted, so craved. It was like he couldn't control himself while in my presence and I loved that. It made me feel sexy, in a way that nothing else ever had.

His hand landed on my shoulder and then he pulled his hips a few inches away from me. I felt him between my legs. He was firm and erect, and I was ready. Without any hesitation, Leo bucked his hips forward, plunging into me. My back arched and my eyes closed as he began to fill me up.

"Oh my God," I groaned, as I took him in.

Leo firmly pressed forward until he was all the way inside. My lips curled into an expression of complete bliss. I reached up and placed my hands on the tile wall of the shower, using it to hold myself up.

God, yes...

My jaw dropped and a squeal of pleasure escaped my lips as Leo began to take me. His powerful body pounded against mine, each thrust causing another wave of pleasure to course through me. The water from the shower poured over us, making our skin slick and creating a soft slapping noise as our bodies collided.

Ecstasy began to fill me, fueled by Leo's thrusts of pleasure. Everything about the moment felt incredible, and it wasn't long before I began rising to orgasm, just as easily as I had at the waterfall.

"Oh my God, Leo," I groaned. "Don't stop."

Leo immediately increased the pace of his thrusts. I pressed back against him, taking him in as deeply as I could. And as my back began to arch further, the pleasure of the orgasm overwhelmed me, launching me into an ecstasy-filled heaven. The sensation was so intense that it took my breath away. A look of lust was frozen on my face; my lips parted and my eyes halfway open. I couldn't believe how fast he had gotten me to climax again.

Leo continued his pace and slid his hand up my back. He grabbed a handful of my wet hair, carefully gripping it near my scalp. I smiled as he tugged it ever so gently, causing my back to arch a little further. The slight change in the position of my body was enough to create a different pleasure, immediately furthering the sensation from my oncoming orgasm.

"Yes..." I moaned, my voice echoing throughout the bedroom-sized shower.

He gave another gentle tug on my hair and then let go, bringing both of his hands to my hips. His grip was strong and steady as he held me, taking me firmly from behind. I wasn't even pushing back against him at that point, because I didn't have to. He had taken total control, guiding me over his cock as he pulled me toward him. All I had to do was hold myself up against the shower wall and let him do as he pleased.

Leo kept that pace for a while and then began to slow down. The intensity of the pleasure hardly changed at all, though. Each slow, methodical thrust filled me, keeping me floating in that state of bliss. My entire body tingled and the wetness between my legs continued to increase. I wanted to tell him how good it felt. But all that I could do is let out a soft moan. My mind was gone, lost somewhere in between the waves of ecstasy and the lust he created.

"Oh, God..." Leo whispered. "You are so damn hot."

He continued his slow pace for just a few more seconds and then he took a step away from me. He placed his hands on my hips and spun me around to face him. I watched as his chest rose and fell in cadence with his breathing, causing his abdominal muscles to flex with the movement.

The desperate throbbing between my legs returned the moment he pulled out and I immediately wanted, *needed,* him back inside of me. The sensual fire in me began to flicker out and the only cure was to have Leo back inside... immediately.

I lifted my hands to his chest, letting my fingers move upward onto his shoulders. Then I softly drew an imaginary line up toward his neck. The stubble on his cheeks tickled my fingertips as I neared his jawline.

Leo was just standing there, breathing heavily as his gaze moved up and down my body. Then he slowly shook his head in awe, as he admired me. He seemed to really love my body, which of course gave me even more sexual self-confidence. And it was that confidence that made me feel like I could really let myself go while having sex with him. And I had to imagine that was part of why the sex was so incredible; I could completely let go.

Not more than a few seconds went by before I lifted the side of my mouth up into a playful smirk as I asked, "Well, what are you waiting for?"

Leo licked his lips and then let out a sexual growl. With his hands on my waist, he stepped forward, pressing my back against the wall of the shower. He was fully erect, throbbing against me as he reached down and grabbed the back of my legs, lifting me off of the tile floor. I let out a playful squeal and placed my hands over his shoulders. Then I wrapped my legs around his waist. He held me up with his powerful arms, putting me in the perfect position to continue our fun.

As he slid into me again, I reached forward and grabbed a handful of his hair. Then I pulled his face toward mine. We kissed, both of us moaning softly as our tongues danced. He held me against the wall and I used my legs to draw him into me, pulling his body against mine. The deep pleasure returned as he filled me up again. With my back pressed against the wall and my hands over his muscular shoulders, he began to pound into me.

Droplets of water landed on his shoulders, and I watched as they slid forward, making their way downward across his chest and into the creases between his washboard abs. Meanwhile, the muscles in his arms flexed as he held me up and pressed me against the wall.

The crazy position created sensations unlike anything I had ever felt. Deep, electrifying pleasure filled me with each of his movements. His manhood created the perfect amount of friction, which sent chills of sensation throughout every part of my body.

My jaw dropped slightly as the pleasure took over once again. I brought my hands to the back of Leo's head, gripping his hair as the ecstasy pulsed inside of me.

"Oh, God," I mouthed, unable to really tell him about the orgasm that was about to rock my body.

The words were barely audible, but loud enough for Leo to hear. He leaned forward, bringing his face to my neck as he increased his pace. I brought my hands to his shoulders, feeling his muscles flex as he moved.

"Don't stop," I said, my words louder this time.

Leo grunted and I could feel as he smiled against my neck. It was pretty clear that he loved making me feel this way. It was almost as if he was more concerned with pleasing me over pleasing himself.

My eyes closed and I rested the back of my head against the wall. Then I drew in a quick breath. At the same time, my body began to tense around him. Frozen in a state of pure nirvana, I let myself ride the wave of orgasm all the way to the peak.

Finally, after a few moments of intensity, the climax faded and I exhaled. Then I slowly opened my eyes and took a few breaths as I regained myself. I couldn't believe it. Leo had sent me to sensory heaven two times in the space of a single shower.

He held his body against mine, slowing his pace to a stop. Then he leaned forward and gently kissed me, teasing me with his lips. I brought my hand up to his face, smiling contentedly as we kissed. My fingers danced down his shoulders, making their way down across his biceps. His skin was slick with moisture, causing my hands to slide easily along.

Leo gently pulled away, breaking our kiss. Then, with one graceful movement, he carried me to the corner of the shower where a tile bench had been installed. I had always just used it to hold the shampoo and conditioner, but I immediately knew what Leo had in mind. He held me up with one arm and then used his other to push the shampoo bottles out of the way. Then he sat me down on the bench. I leaned back against the wall and spread my legs apart as I ushered him toward me.

His feet were on the floor of the shower, putting him at the perfect elevation to resume our intimacy. Steam from the hot water surrounded him, making it so that I could only see his silhouette against the glass shower door behind him. He took a step toward me and lifted my legs, draping my knees over his shoulders.

"I just can't get enough of you," he said as he plunged back inside of me.

I gasped as a pulse of pleasure shot through me. Leo then leaned forward and brought his lips to mine, kissing me deeply as we continued making love. His powerful body pressed into mine, pounding me firmly yet sensually. It felt incredible and it made it seem like my second orgasm hadn't even ended.

Leo began to increase the pace of his thrusts, breaking our kiss. I reached my hands above my head, letting the water rain over my front as I relaxed back against the wall. He kept pace for a few minutes, filling both of us with extreme pleasure. Then suddenly, I watched as he began to breathe harder than before. And it was only a moment later when the expression on his face began to change.

I didn't need him to speak to know exactly what he was

thinking. And I needed all of him inside of me. I nodded my head and whispered, "Please..."

Leo closed his eyes and continued his pace. A few seconds later, a soft grunt escaped his lips and I could tell that he was climaxing. I reached forward and pulled him toward me, pulling him deeper inside me.

With my hands around his back, I held his body against me, savoring the last moments of sex. Then I slowly dropped my hands, allowing him to pull out. A contented smile crossed my face. The desperation between my legs had finally ceased and all that was left was a lingering pleasure and a feeling of satiation.

Leo took a step back and I brought my feet to the floor. I glanced around, noticing that the steam had completely filled the shower and I could hardly see to the other side.

"Come here," Leo said, as he reached forward, taking my hands in his.

He helped me to my feet and then grabbed my hips, pulling me in for a kiss. This time, though, the kiss was much more sensual and there was already a smile on my face as I gently pulled away from him.

We stood there for a moment, our breathing finally slowing down to a normal pace. Then Leo flashed a playful smile.

"This is officially the best shower *ever*," he said.

I laughed. "Now you're really never leaving, right?"

He nuzzled the sweet spot right under my ear, making me shiver with delight. "Never, ever."

"So, you said something about a boat ride?" I asked, leaning against the shower wall. "Wait, which one? I'm not getting on that death trap you call a boat," I said firmly. "Besides, you promised you wouldn't use it."

"Whoa- I'm not talking about *that* boat." Leo held up his hands defensively. "I have other boats. I don't know if you knew this, but I am a billionaire."

"So, which one?" I crossed my arms, feeling the water pool between my breasts.

"*Silver Lightning*." His mouth was smug, knowing that I couldn't object to this boat. It was a luxury speed boat that had been in several movies. She had the ability to fly across the water so smoothly it was like sailing on glass. Plus, she was safe.

"I like that boat," I said, grinning. I had been on it before, back when Leo first purchased it.

"You sure it's not too fast for you?" Leo asked, putting a reassuring hand on my shoulder. "I might be able to get you a row boat..."

"I can handle it." I shrugged my shoulder to remove his patronizing hand. "Can I drive?"

"No." Leo shook his head, his expression flat.

I crossed my arms and pouted.

"Maybe," he relented, the corners of his lips slightly turning up. I grinned.

Leo went to the shower door and stepped out, grabbing a white fluffy towel from the towel rack. "I'll go grab us some coffee. You take your time and finish your shower."

I nodded, watching as his perfect body disappeared under fluffy towel. I wished there was a way to dry off that didn't involve a towel. I could have him naked all the time and be content. Maybe I'd invest in a big blow dryer...

Leo flashed me one last grin before heading into the bedroom to get dressed. I stood under the warm water, letting my shoulders relax and just smiling at how happy I was.

With a laugh, I picked up my razor, realizing that I just had fantastic sex without shaving my legs first. If that wasn't true love, then what the hell was?

15

———

I was just finishing putting on my sundress over my swimsuit when Leo came back in to my bedroom. He was still wearing the same clothes from yesterday, but he looked amazing. He held out the steaming mug of coffee for me and I took a nice long sip.

Two creams, extra sweet. Just the way I liked it.

"Do we need to stop at your place and pick you up anything?" I asked, eyeing the mashed potato mark on his shirt.

"I have a change of clothes and a swimsuit on the boat," he told me. He grinned. "As long as you don't mind me changing in front of you."

I put my hands to my cheeks. "Oh! The scandal!"

Leo laughed and held out his hand for mine. "You ready?"

I nodded, finishing off the last of my coffee and grabbing my bag.

Leo opened the door and scanned the hallway, shaking his head. "I keep thinking I'm doing something bad. That

Bastian is going to jump out at any moment and demand payment for your honor."

"Payment for my honor?" I giggled. "I knew you were charming, but I was unaware you were a knight of the round table."

Leo rolled his eyes at me and pulled me out into the hallway. I glanced around, expecting Bastian to appear at any moment and listening for the slightest creak.

I had always been a good kid in high school. I didn't sneak out, I wasn't into parties or goofing off with boys, but now I knew the rush that it gave. I could suddenly see why it was so much fun to sneak out of the house.

"I like being bad with you," I whispered as we paused at the bottom of the stairs before dashing to the front door. "We should be bad more often."

Outside the air was already beginning to heat with the day. It was the perfect day for being out on the water. Here on the island it would only get more humid and hot as the sun rose overhead, but out on the water, it would be perfect. A blue sky and dark water with the wind blowing in our hair was exactly what I needed for a day off.

Murdoch silently followed behind us. The only reason I even noticed he was there was that I was specifically looking for him. My own bodyguard, Eli, was probably enjoying having Murdoch watch me. It was practically like a day off for Eli, too.

Leo took my hand as we followed the path to the beach and began the easy walk to the docks. Granted, it was a longer walk following the pretty white sand, but much more romantic. The sky was a cloudless blue that stretched out for as far as I could see. Blue water rolled steadily in toward the land, slowly growing lighter until it was clear upon the sand. Gulls called down to us as they hovered over the waves waiting for something to eat.

"Look at that sand castle." Leo pointed to an elaborate creation not far from the beach. It was far enough inland that the tides hadn't destroyed it yet. It was definitely the work of adults rather than children playing in the sand.

"I could live in a sand castle," I mused, looking at the shells placed carefully for decoration.

"There would be sand everywhere," Leo remarked. "In the kitchen, in the living room, on the couch, in the bed..."

I giggled. "It's not like you ever have to clean it."

"Yeah, but that doesn't mean I don't like it." Leo made a face and tugged on my hand. "Maybe we'll make one of those later today. But not one you can live in."

My steps easily matched his as we continued down to the marina where most of the island's resident billionaires kept their boats. It wasn't the biggest marina I'd ever seen, but it definitely was worth the most. Multi-million dollar yachts floated and bobbed next to speed boats that were worth a small country.

"Ahoy there, Leo," called out a friendly voice. A handsome mane of sandy-blond hair popped up over the top of one of the beautiful sailing yachts. "Hey, Charlotte!"

Leo dropped my hand. While neither one of us was quite ready to break the news to everyone that we were a couple, I was still disappointed that he was willing to hide it so quickly. I understood, though. My older brother was rather protective and he and Leo worked together. We had to announce it carefully.

Still, I hated losing his hand. Our relationship didn't feel as real, like it could still all be in my head, without having his touch to prove it.

"Hi, Robbie," I called back, recognizing Robbie Saunders as the man hailing us. He was Jack's younger brother and an expert sailor. He had won more races in a sailboat than I had ever heard of even existing.

"You getting on that death trap you call a boat?" Robbie asked, leaning against the railing of his boat and grinning down at us. The two Saunders boys had similar builds and coloring, but couldn't be more different. Where Jack was a businessman through and through, Robbie was wild and free. Until recently, he had been a bit of a problem for the Saunders' family.

"Hi, Robbie," Leo greeted the man, rolling his eyes. Robbie loved sailing with sails where Leo liked going fast using an engine.

"You know, Charlotte, you can come sailing with us. You might actually live," Robbie teased, grinning out at us from his boat like a Cheshire cat.

"Ha ha, very funny," Leo replied, crossing his arms.

"Give me a good sailing boat over one of those racers any day," Robbie said. "Those things are nuts."

"Oh, come on, Robbie," Leo replied in a good-natured tone. "You're telling me you've never thought about trying to break the water speed record? I know you like to go fast."

"Not that fast." Robbie shook his head. "I have no desire to go so fast that I'm hydroplaning and praying I don't slam into the water at 300 mph because I hit a wave wrong. If we were supposed to go that fast on the water, we'd be able to do it with sails."

As if to prove his point on the danger, a wave knocked his boat gently and made him grab the railing.

"Besides, if I want to go fast, I can get in a car and break 300 without breaking a sweat. " Robbie continued. "Give me a sailboat any day. That requires skill and you might actually live."

"You have no sense of adventure, Robbie." Leo shook his head and clicked his tongue. "You can't break records if you're afraid of a little risk."

"A little risk?" Robbie scoffed. "An eighty-five percent fatality rate of everyone whose ever attempted to break the record isn't risk. That's not sport. That's a suicide attempt."

"I agree," I added quietly. I'd seen the boats Leo liked to race. They skittered over the water like jet fueled bugs, barely clinging to the surface and liable to go flying at the smallest wave. They were million-dollar deathmobiles of speed.

"Just because I'm in a boat that can go that fast doesn't mean I am," Leo replied calmly. "I haven't gotten anywhere near the 317 mph record. And I have no intention of trying to."

"But you're on a boat that is designed to do that," I said, trying to get my fears across to him. "You like to push limits. How long before you go just a little too fast because your boat can handle it but you can't?"

Leo's eyes flashed. This argument was far from over.

"Oh, hey, Charlotte and Leo!" A female voice interjected, stopping whatever Leo's retort was going to be. "I thought I heard voices up here."

Sam, or rather Samantha, came to join her husband at the railing. Her sun-bleached blonde hair was pulled back out of her tanned smiling face. She was the reason that Robbie was no longer a problem child. He wrapped his arm around her shoulder and she leaned into him like he was her strength. Robbie's caressed her arm as he pulled her closer to him. It was such a small motion, but it spoke of a deep love between them.

I envied them slightly. They spent their days either racing sailboats or teaching others how to sail. They got to be with the love of their life doing the thing that they loved most. I hoped Leo and I could be that happy someday.

"Hi, Sam," I greeted her. "It's good to see you."

Leo murmured an appropriate greeting as well. Our discussion on the safety of his boat would have to wait until later.

"So, we're planning a little outing this evening for friends. Just floating around the island a bit. You two are more than welcome to join us," Sam offered. "Right now, it's the two of us, Jack and Emma, and hopefully you two."

"Thank you," I answered slowly, looking over at Leo to make sure I wasn't getting our plans wrong. "I'm not sure what our plans are, but we'll keep you in mind."

"Sounds good. No pressure." Sam smiled and leaned into Robbie, putting her head on his shoulder. "It looks like you are off to go have an adventure. Have fun!"

"Thanks," Leo and I chorused. We all waved as Leo and I continued down the dock to where he had the *Silver Lightning* docked.

Leo hopped into the open cockpit and pulled out a set of keys. Unlocking a panel in the back, he pulled out a pair of swim trunks and tossed them to me. "Hold on to these for me."

I laughed, climbing in to the passenger seat and settling in. The tan seats were soft to the touch, even though I knew they had to be waterproof. It even had what looked like mahogany trim, giving the boat a classic and elegant feel. Every detail of this boat was made for the very rich, and then I knew Leo had tricked it out.

He turned the key in the ignition and the engine purred to life. This boat could go fast. Not breaking the record for a vehicle on water kind of fast, but definitely fast enough to give me a thrill.

Leo grinned at me as he maneuvered the boat carefully out of the dock and out toward open water. As soon as we hit the buoy marking freedom, he gunned it. I slammed into the back of my seat, laughing as the waves sped by and my hair streamed out behind me.

Leo was an expert driver. He had to be in order to pilot the boat I refused to even think of. But now he was using those skills to show off.

Twisting through the water like a powerful sea creature, the *Silver Lightning* ran the waves. I loved the way the wind blew through my hair and the sound of the ocean caressing our boat as we sped along. I had no idea where we were going, but I didn't care. If all we did was drive around in a boat all day, I would consider that a perfect day with Leo.

Leo slowed the boat and then turned off the engine. My ears throbbed with the sudden silence.

"So, you still have that swim suit for me?" he asked, turning to look at me.

I hastily stuck it under my leg. "Nope. Threw it overboard."

"Right." Leo stared at my legs and then back up to my face with a raised eyebrow. "I guess we're going skinny dipping, then."

"Skinny dipping?" I repeated. That was definitely one of my fantasies. Of course, it was usually at the lake by the university campus, but that was beside the point. My heart fluttered and I couldn't stop the giddy feeling.

I'd already kissed him. I'd already had sex with him. Hell, technically, we already went skinny-dipping in the waterfall, but I couldn't help it. I wanted this. He just had the ability to tangle me up and make me want everything with him.

"You up for it?" Leo asked, stripping off his shirt and

revealing his torso. His muscles flexed with the movement and it was hard not to stare. "Or are you afraid a mermaid might see you?"

I narrowed my eyes. "You should be more worried about a *merman*," I corrected. "Because I know what my body does to you. Imagine what it would do to a poor fish boy."

I pulled my dress up over my head, enjoying the way Leo's eyes popped out a little. Knowing that he found me sexually appealing was a total turn on. Every girl doubts their own beauty, so seeing the man I adored so thoroughly engrossed and excited by me, I could believe him that I was beautiful. I believed him straight to the core of my being. In Leo's eyes, I was perfect. I was beautiful.

Slowly, I undid my bikini top, keeping myself covered but loving the way his eyes dilated as he watched. With a grin, I finally tossed it to the floor and stood there proudly.

"Are you trying to skip the swimming all together?" he growled, his voice deep and full of desire. If I hadn't believed that he wanted me before, the sound of his voice convinced me entirely. It was primal and needy.

"Maybe..." I glanced over the edge of the boat into the dark waters. "Maybe I'm just afraid of sharks."

Leo's eyes flashed with dark heat that made his blue irises shine. "Then best not risk it..."

He dropped his shorts, kicking them to the side so he was completely and gloriously naked in front of me.

"Leo!" I cried, flirtatiously.

He immediately shrugged his shoulders and flashed his boyish smile.

"What?" he asked, with innocence in his voice. "We're in the middle of nowhere. There's not another person for miles. You said you wanted to be bad more often, right?"

It was definitely a good point. I quickly glanced around

the harbor. There wasn't a soul in sight. The speed at which he had driven the boat away from the docks had gained us quite a distance in a short amount of time. I brought my gaze back to Leo, noticing that he had already become mostly erect.

"If there is a merman out there in the water, let's give him a show," he said.

His eyes never left my body and I slowly let my hands drop, revealing my bare chest. Anybody on the shore with a pair of binoculars could have seen us standing there, but in that moment, it didn't really concern me. And besides, a part of me almost *liked* the fact that maybe someone could see us if they wanted to.

"You are *so* bad," I whispered, shaking my head at him.

Leo knew it, too. And he knew I liked it when he was just a little bad. He knew that it turned me on more than anything and that I wouldn't be able to help myself. My eyes lifted, meeting his. His pupils were still dilated as he took a step closer to me, closing the gap between us. A burst of excitement filled me as he placed his hands on my sides, just under my ribs but above my hips, pulling me close.

"You're kind of bad yourself," he said with a half-smile. "Maybe that's why I like you so much."

As soon as he finished speaking, he brought his face toward mine. I stood on my tiptoes and kissed him, feeling a pleasurable tingle fill my body as our lips touched. He had become completely erect and as I leaned close I could feel him slide between my legs. My bikini bottoms were still on, but it didn't matter. There was still enough friction to create a light pleasure.

Leo's hands dropped a bit further, landing on my hips. His fingers grazed over the waist strap of my bikini bottoms as we kissed and I felt him slide his fingers into the knots that held them together on the sides. Just one small pull of the strings and the bikini bottoms would drop, rendering me completely naked and ready. But I wanted to tease him a little bit before we got into it. So I gently took a step back, causing his hands to fall from my hips.

"Sit down," I ordered, with a playful smile on my face.

Leo cocked his head to the side, but smiled as he played along. He sat down on the leather Captain's seat, then swiveled it so that he was facing me. His manhood stood proudly in his lap, ready to pleasure me.

I placed my hands over his shoulders and then crawled on top of him, straddling his lap. He let out a moan and leaned his head back as my body dragged over his sensitive parts.

"Oh my God," he whispered.

He placed his hands on my hips, once again going for the knots to untie the bikini bottoms. And once again, I gently pulled away.

"Nuh uh," I said, shaking my head.

Leo's jaw dropped slightly and his breath began to quicken. I could tell that I was turning him on and I loved it. It made me feel so sexy that I could turn on a man like Leo with nothing more than a few subtle movements.

"You're killin' me," he groaned.

He reached forward, placing his hands on my butt and pulling me further on top of him. Then he brought his face to my breasts, giving them attention with his tongue. My lips parted and I drew in a deep breath as his touch shot a burst of pleasure into my body. I instantly became wet with desire, ready to have him inside of me.

While he kissed my breasts, he moved his hands back down to the knots at my waist. This time, however, I didn't stop him. I kept my arms wrapped over his shoulders, straddling him as he pulled at the strings. Both sides came loose at the same time and I gently lifted my body up, just enough so that Leo could pull my swimsuit bottoms away. He then tossed them carelessly to the floor of the boat. His hands immediately went back to my ass, which was now completely bare. All I had to do was drop my weight and he would slide inside, easing the throbbing desperation between my legs.

"You are trouble," I said, smiling. "Pure trouble."

Leo licked his lips as he brought his gaze up and down my body. I started to drop my weight, sinking down over him. But he stopped me immediately.

"Nuh uh," he said, imitating the words that I had spoken just seconds before.

I playfully slapped him on the shoulder.

"Leo!" I said. "You can't do that!"

My body had anticipated having him inside of me and when that didn't happen, the desperation between my legs increased even further. Leo bit his bottom lip sexually and then wrapped his arms around the underside of my thighs. Then he stood up, carrying me a few steps over to my chair and setting me down on it. I leaned back, feeling the warm leather as it touched my back. I gently spread my legs, bringing them around his waist and ushering him to come closer. He bucked his hips forward just enough so that he began to enter me. Then he pulled away, with a smirk on his face.

"Two can play at this game," he said.

My mouth dropped in shock and I felt the wetness increase between my legs. Something about the way he was teasing me turned me on so much.

"You are just plain mean," I responded jokingly.

Leo took a step back and then dropped to his knees in

front of me, disappearing from view. He draped my legs over his shoulders, keeping his strong hands on the top of my waist. I felt his facial stubble tickle the skin on the inside of my thighs as he leaned forward, bringing his face to my flower.

"Yes..." I whispered.

As soon as his mouth met me, an electric shock of sensation burst into my body. I leaned my head back and closed my eyes as Leo delicately flicked pleasure into me with his lips and tongue.

"Oh my," I mouthed.

No sound came out of me, though. The pleasure had rendered me speechless. The way that Leo moved his mouth was so gentle and tender, teasing my most sensitive parts with just the right amount of pressure. Slowly but surely, my body filled with ecstasy, each lap of his tongue bringing me closer to the point of climax.

I drew in a quick breath as I became frozen in sensation, unable to think or move. Leo lapped one more time and then gently pulled away. My frozen state of bliss suddenly vanished and I opened my eyes immediately. At the same time, I reached forward with both hands and grabbed the top of his hair, pulling his face back into me.

"Not yet," I groaned. "You're not done yet."

Leo let out a soft, sexual growl. The sound vibrated into me as he resumed the work with his mouth. The pleasure returned, this time with even more intensity. It only took a few moments before I rose to orgasm once again.

"Don't stop," I whispered, as I gently held his face against me.

And he didn't stop. He didn't even slow down. He kept his pace, easing his lips against my body and darting his tongue out in just the right way to put me over the top. I writhed on the leather chair as a final wave of pleasure filled me. My thighs were clamped around his head as my body shuddered with heavenly bliss.

I gently leaned my head back and reminded myself to breathe. Then I relaxed my legs, letting Leo pull away. After a moment of regaining my senses, I sat up in the chair and looked down to Leo. A look of lust was on his face as he stood up from the floor. I immediately wrapped my legs around his waist and pulled him close to me.

"You're incredible," I said, as I let my fingers drag over my chest.

Leo's eyes moved over my body and he shook his head in awe.

"So are you," he responded.

The pace of his breathing had increased and the movement caused the muscles in his chest and abs to flex in cadence. The sun beat down on us and I noticed a light layer of sweat covering his skin, accentuating his defined body even further and making me want him even more.

"No more teasing," I begged, before gently biting my bottom lip.

Leo placed his hands onto the top of the seat and leaned forward. He held his body over mine, making me feel tiny against his muscular frame. My legs were wrapped around his waist, and all I had to do was pull his body against me to get exactly what I wanted. It made me feel like I was in control. I lifted my hands and brought them to his face, leaning toward him for a kiss. At the same time, I used my legs to pull him into me, drawing him deep into my sex.

My jaw dropped as he filled me ecstasy, inch by inch. The frantic throbbing in my groin finally ceased and all that was left was a deep, contented pleasure. Leo pulled away from our kiss and began bucking his hips forward, pounding me against the chair. My lips curled up into an expression of euphoria, which might have looked more like a goofy smile, but I couldn't help it. The intense sensation that filled me made it impossible to control.

His hands gripped the top of the chair as we made love. I watched as his expression became focused, his eyes squinting and his jaw flexing. He began to thrust into me rhythmically, using his entire body to pleasure me. It was a like a dance, a perfect dance. I brought my hands to my chest, drawing circles over the sensitive parts of my breasts as Leo continued his pace.

Suddenly, a light breeze blew across the boat, tossing my hair across my face. The boat rocked a bit as well as a small wave rose underneath us. It did nothing to stop Leo's passionate thrusts, though. In fact, he began to increase his pace, causing me to squirm in delight on the hot leather seat.

Our bodies became intertwined. My hands moved up and down his back and my legs were wrapped tightly around his waist. His chest hovered over mine and the heat from his skin radiated downward, covering my body. My breasts bounced in cadence with his movements, the points of pleasure on top dragging along his pectorals, sending pleasurable shivers into me that only added to the elixir of sensation.

I relaxed back into the seat, closing my eyes and letting Leo take me as he pleased. I could feel his breathing, as his exhalations cooled my sweat-covered skin. The moment felt so perfect, that I didn't really want it to ever end. The beautiful scenery, both in and out of the boat, combined with the intimate connection that Leo and I were sharing. It was perfect.

After a moment, I opened my eyes and brought my

hands to Leo's forearms, feeling the muscles ripple underneath my fingertips as he took me completely. A look of lust was on his face, with his eyes half-opened and his lips parted. He looked like he was experiencing the same heavenly bliss that I was.

After a few more seconds, he slowed his pace down. There was a look in his eyes that told me that he wanted more, something else from me. I knew exactly what it was and I was happy to give it to him.

"You want me from behind?" I asked, innocently.

Leo smiled as he caught his breath, his chest heaving. He was so lost in pleasure, though, that he couldn't even speak. He simply nodded in agreement and took a step back, immediately creating a void inside of me that he had been filling. So I quickly stood up from the chair and stepped over to the metal railing on the side of the boat. Then I bent over in front of him.

He didn't hesitate for a second. He positioned himself behind me and placed his hands on my hips. Then he plunged back in, causing me to gasp in pleasure. I held onto the railing as he took me from behind, pounding me even harder than before.

In the far distance, I could see the shoreline and I instantly smiled at the thought of someone standing out there with a pair of binoculars. I knew it was so naughty, but the idea definitely continued to turn me on. We didn't want anyone to know that we were together, yet here we were, making love for all to see. I loved it.

With his hands firmly gripping my hips, he pulled my body into his, causing him to slide in deeper and harder. The increased pressure pumped more waves of ecstasy into me and an uncontrollable squeal of pleasure escaped my lips. Our bodies rocked against each other's and our moist skin created a soft slapping noise that bounced along the water.

I could tell by his change in pace that he was nearing climax. His movements became even more focused and quick, slipping deeper which each thrust. My moans became louder, and I knew that just spurred him on to the finish. A moment later, Leo pressed against mine and let out a loud groan. He climaxed hard and deep, releasing himself into me just the way that I wanted him to.

He kept his hands my hips for a second longer and then slowly released me. Then he took a step back, causing his manhood to fall away. I immediately turned around to face him. He was panting hard, as he recovered. I stepped close and placed my hands on to his chest, feeling his heart beat underneath my fingertips.

"That was amazing," I said, as I drew circles over his pecks with my fingers.

Leo took a few more breaths and then wrapped his arms around me, gently kissing me on the lips. When he pulled away, he flashed his boyish smile and responded, "I'd say the merman got the show that he was hoping for."

I playfully slapped him on the shoulder.

"Come on," I said. "Let's go skinny dipping now. I need to cool off."

16

———

"We should probably head back," I murmured, not wanting to move. The sun was hot and the boat was rocking me back to sleep, but it was Leo that I was enjoying. Cuddled up together in the back of his boat, I was getting to touch every inch of him. I had him all to myself and I didn't want this to end.

"You're right," Leo agreed, but didn't move either.

My stomach grumbled and then Leo's answered.

"Well, I can't have you going hungry," Leo said, slowly untangling my limbs from his. I sighed, but enjoyed the view as he got up. The man had a very impressive ass, especially from this angle. "Where are my shorts?"

"In the seat," I informed him, slowly coming to standing myself. It took me a moment to locate my swim suit and pull the sundress back down over my body.

"I really wish we could just be nudists." Leo grinned as he watched me dress. "But then, I'd never get anything done. Just you."

"I think I could handle being the only thing on your

schedule," I replied, doing my best to use a sultry voice. I wasn't sure I was pulling it off, but the way Leo's eyes heated told me I was doing a decent job.

He took a step toward me and put his hand on my neck, pulling me into a kiss. "You come to my office, I'll certainly put you on my schedule. And my desk. And my chair..." his words faded as his lips met mine. He tasted like sunshine with just a hint of salt.

Dirty jokes and kisses. This is what heaven looked like.

My stomach rumbled again. *Well, at least pretty close to heaven*, I amended in my head.

Leo released me from his kiss and it took me a moment to regain my balance. With any other person, I would have blamed the boat for making me lightheaded, but with Leo, I knew better. He made my heart sing and my body react in ways I'd never experienced before.

The ride back to the docks was quick. The noise of the engine and the wind made it hard to hold a conversation, so we just held hands and watched the ocean disappear under our boat. The island quickly came back into view, and for a moment I let myself pretend we were on a deserted island. That there were no people, no jobs, no responsibilities to take us away from one another ever again.

I'd never wished for anything so hard in my life.

Leo pulled the *Silver Lightning* into the empty stall next to his racing boat. I glared at the red painted monstrosity next to me. The words, *Speed Demon* printed in bright yellow mocked all decent thoughts of safety. I hated that boat so much.

"Mr. Westbrook."

I looked up to see Toby, Leo's personal assistant, waiting for us on the docks. I was so busy trying to sink the *Speed Demon* with my eyes that I hadn't even noticed him.

It didn't help that Toby, with his short, pudgy stature, floppy brown hair, and unassuming posture was easy to overlook.

"Toby? What are you doing here?" Leo asked, cutting power to the engine and tossing him a rope. I had gone on enough boat outings to know how to help tie up, so I grabbed a rope and assisted.

"I'm very sorry, sir, but there's a matter that needs your attention." Toby fidgeted slightly, pulling at his dress collar. He was wearing dark blue suit slacks and I could see the matching suit jacket hanging off a bench. Unfortunately, I could also see a very large white bird poop squarely on the arm of the dark jacket.

"What do you mean, Toby?" Leo asked, confused. "Is this about the new phone app?"

"No, sir," Toby said slowly. His brown eyes skittered over to me and then back to his boss. "It's about the other thing."

Leo stilled, his hands stopped in mid knot. "I thought that was taken care of." There was an edge to his voice that made me nervous.

"I'm afraid not, Leo." Toby shifted his feet. I wondered if he had a fear of the ocean. He was never nervous at the office or on the phone, but today he seemed out of sorts. Maybe it was just the heat of wearing a full dress suit in the Caribbean sun, maybe it was whatever thing he and Leo were talking about, but the man was off.

Leo finished tying off the boat and sighed. "Charlotte, I hate to do this to you, but I need to take care of this."

"So no lunch?" I tried really hard not to pout. This was my day off and I didn't get many. I had been looking forward to spending the entire day with Leo.

"I'm afraid not." Leo's blue eyes held a shadow of fear that I'd never seen before, but then he blinked and it was gone. "I promise I'll make it up to you, though. Best lunch ever."

"All right," I said reluctantly. "As long as you promise."

Leo smiled, the sparkle coming back to his eyes. I took a step forward, wanting to kiss him, but he subtly shook his head. His eyes darted over toward Toby and he frowned.

"Right." I understood that. Not in front of Toby. I sighed. I wondered if we'd ever go public. I wanted to tell the world that Leo was finally mine, but he was being so damn careful not to tell a soul. Did he really want me- or was he just stringing me along as an easy thing?

"I'm sorry, Charlotte," Toby replied, not sounding sorry at all. I wanted to hit him. Not only was Toby taking my boyfriend away, but he was unwittingly denying me a goodbye kiss. I hoped that what ever the two of them had to deal with was worth it.

"Do you need any help?" I asked, hoping that maybe we could spend some time together that way.

"No!" Leo's response was almost too quick. "I mean, it's not business related. This is a personal thing. Just some purchases and such."

"Uh huh." I didn't believe him, but I wasn't about to call him out for it. Both Leo and Toby looked far too glum and nervous for it not to be a serious problem. "Okay. Maybe I'll see you later?"

"I'd like that," Leo assured me. He paused, obviously wanting to kiss me goodbye, but still not wanting to show our relationship to Toby. He stuffed his hands in his pockets. "I'll see you later, Charlotte."

I wasn't sure what to think of this whole situation. It felt off in a way I couldn't describe. Something was going on with Toby and Leo, and it stung a little that Leo didn't want to share with me. I sighed. *Leo must have his reasons*, I thought. *I just wish I knew what they were.* I'd just need to trust Leo. I'd trusted him most of my life, I could trust him on this.

Even if it felt like something dark was going on.

And with that, he turned and walked off the docks with Toby.

17

I stepped off of the Saunders' sailboat and then turned around and waved goodbye. Since Leo had ditched me to go take care of his problem, I had decided to take Robbie and Sam up on their offer to go sailing for the evening.

It had turned out to be a wonderful way to spend the day. It would have been better if Leo had been there, but I was trying very hard not to complain. I'd lived without Leo in my every waking moment this long, I was sure I could handle it a little bit longer.

So, I had done my best to be social. And really, being with Robbie, Sam, Emma, and Jack was a good way to spend the evening. We had sailed around the island, enjoying the sights and being out on the water using only the wind to power us. It was so different that powering across the water in a speed boat- more relaxed.

The sky was slowly turning dark purple as the sun slid beneath her dark ocean blanket. The crickets were starting their noisy chorus and the temperature was now perfect. I took a deep breath of warm air and let it out slowly. A motion out of the corner of my eye caught my attention.

"Hi, Elijah," I greeted the man hiding in the shadows of a bush. He wasn't trying to be stealthy, just unobtrusive. I greatly appreciated that Eli always did his best to try and let Bastian and I have the illusion that we weren't always being followed. I knew of other bodyguards that loomed over their clients at all times, and while sometimes appropriate, I much preferred Eli's discrete practices.

"Good evening, Charlotte," Elijah said, stepping out of the shadows. He was a big man with dark features. He often reminded me of a hunting lion in the way that he moved, not to mention that he was just as deadly.

"I'm going to walk home through town," I told him. "Will you walk with me so I don't feel like I'm being stalked like a deer?"

Elijah chuckled and nodded. "Of course. Why through town though? It's a longer walk."

"Because if you're here, then that means Bastian and Ava are safely tucked away at the mansion," I said, starting to walk toward the main road through town. "And they should have a little privacy."

"Yes, it is hard to find a private space with only 14 bedrooms," Elijah said, rolling his eyes.

I let out a long frustrated sigh and considered telling him to just go back to stalking me.

We walked in silence. I found that I enjoyed his company a lot more when we weren't talking. Night was falling and the street lamps and store lights lit the road through town. We passed Adele's restaurant and the bar and shops beside it, continuing to walk past a small grocery store. At the end of the block, before my turn to head home was the community center and church.

The open door of the church was a bright light against the surrounding darkness. It made a pretty picture to look at before turning. The door to the community center was open as well with people exiting and hurrying to their cars. I was about to keep walking, but one of the people leaving caught my eye. It was a form that I had spent much of my life looking for. Leo.

I stopped on the path, still too far from the community center to be seen. Elijah took an extra step before turning to look at me like I was crazy for stopping. I stared over at the community center, trying to figure out what Leo was doing there. I knew that it couldn't be for business, not with that many people and no mention of it on Bastian's schedule.

Then, Toby came out of the building and joined Leo. They waved to a man heading into the church before heading to the parking lot themselves.

"Do you know what's going on at the community center?" I asked Elijah, thinking maybe there was some sort of town hall meeting or something. Something that would be important enough for Leo to not call me.

"What am I? A social calendar?" Elijah's sarcasm was not what I needed.

I recognized Murdoch, Leo's incredibly scary bodyguard, driving the car that Leo and Toby were getting in to. Murdoch revved the engine and the three of them drove off into the night. I stared after them for a moment.

What in the world were they doing here? What were they doing that was so important? Did it have anything to do with Leo's departure this afternoon?

I set my shoulders and hurried across the street. I trusted Leo, but I needed to know what was going on. I was sure he had a good reason for everything that had happened today, but I still felt a little left out.

"Where are you going?" Elijah asked, jogging to catch up with my sudden departure. "What are you doing?"

"There's a sign on the door," I said, waving him off. "I'll be right back."

Elijah made a frustrated noise but fell back slightly as I approached the door to the community center. I took a deep breath and stepped close enough to read the paper.

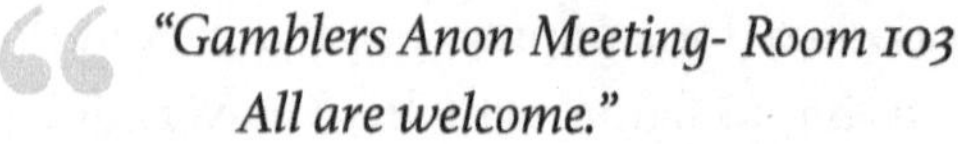

"Gamblers Anon Meeting- Room 103
All are welcome."

I HAD to laugh at myself. I was worried over nothing. He wasn't being strange or leaving me out of his life. He was making sure that he didn't gamble. That he stayed true to himself. If anything, I should be proud of him.

That Toby was there at the meeting as well told me that Toby was probably a gambler. I felt a little guilty, discovering a secret that wasn't mine to know. I didn't know Toby all that well. I had helped train him when Leo first hired him, and I helped him out from time to time, but I wouldn't call us friends. I would barely call us co-workers, to be honest. Knowing something this personal about him without his consent was slightly uncomfortable.

I supposed that it was possible for Toby to just be there as support for Leo, but I doubted it. If Leo wanted someone for support, he could have just brought me. I knew his secret now. No, it made more sense that they were both members.

I let out a long breath. There was no way for me to unlearn that information, so the best thing I could do is just keep it a secret. I was the assistant to a billionaire, it wasn't like keeping secrets was hard for me. Besides, Leo obviously knew Toby's past and that would be my only concern anyway.

If anything, it made me love Leo a little bit more.

I took out my phone and texted him.

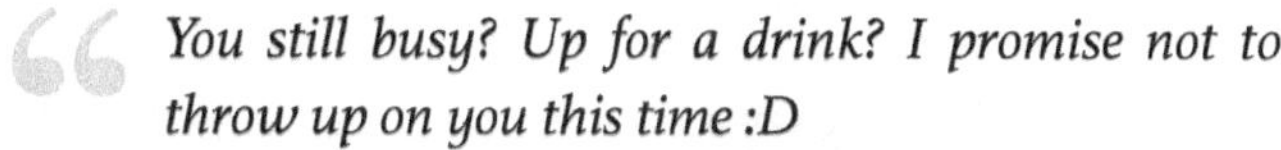

You still busy? Up for a drink? I promise not to throw up on you this time :D

I TURNED from the door and headed back to the sidewalk where Elijah was waiting for me with his arms crossed.

"Figure it all out?" Elijah asked.

I nodded as my phone buzzed with a reply from Leo.

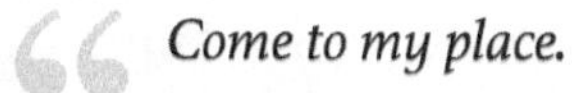

Come to my place.

"CHANGE OF PLANS, Eli- I'm going to Leo's," I said with a grin, putting my phone in my pocket.

THE WALK to Leo's from the community center wasn't far. He was staying at a big place on the water that actually belonged to a friend of his. Owen Parker was a good friend to both Leo and Jack Saunders, and let any of his billionaire friends use the beautiful seaside mansion whenever they were on the island.

I loved the big, white, marble columns and old British colony look of the place. A security guard called out a greeting to us, recognizing Elijah as we approached.

"So, are you two a thing now?" Elijah asked as we walked toward the house. "I mean, officially?"

I nearly tripped on the smooth walkway. "Maybe..."

"So you *are,*" he said with a grin. I gave him a dirty look and he just smiled bigger. "Murdoch owes me twenty bucks."

"Why would Murdoch owe you twenty bucks?" I asked, taking the first step to the main doors. "What did you bet on?"

"That the two of you would get together," Elijah answered with a shrug, pulling on the big door and holding it open for me. "Murdoch's a cynic and didn't think it would happen. He bet that you two would never be a couple."

"Seriously?" I asked. I had always thought that Murdoch liked me, but that fact that he was betting that Leo and I would never be together made my heart sink. Why didn't he think we would make it? I paused. "But, you bet that we would be a couple?"

"Yeah." Elijah said with a grin. "I always bet on love."

18

———

Once inside the mansion, I turned to go up the curving staircase to the master bedroom while Elijah veered off to the kitchen to find Murdoch and get his money.

The stairs echoed with the clicks of my steps as I ran up them and threw open the doors to the big bedroom. The balcony doors leading to the ocean were open, letting in the warm night air filled with the scent of the ocean. Leo was at his desk, poring over something and frowning. The room was dark except for the light on his desk and the blue glow from his computer screen.

"You okay?" I asked, coming over to him. He had his hand on his head like he was in pain and there were shadows in his eyes that hadn't been there this morning. "Leo is something wrong with the phone app? Do I need to get Bastian?"

"No, no need for Bastian. Everything's fine." He closed the lid to his laptop and gave me a weak smile.

"Are you sure? It's not a problem, Leo." My concern grew a little. His voice was just too hollow and it felt like a lie.

"It's just something I need Murdoch to look into for me. That's all." He sighed, standing up from the desk. The thought of Murdoch looking into something gave me shivers. I wouldn't want to be on the other end of anything but a smile from Murdoch, and even that still was dangerous. Murdoch was a great bodyguard, but he was scary.

"You look great by the way," Leo said, changing the subject.

"What? I haven't done anything special..." I ran a hand over my hair, noting that it was still windblown and tangled from sailing.

Leo came around the desk, pulling me into him with an arm around my hips. He looked down at me like I was the most beautiful thing he'd ever seen.

"You're all windswept and your cheeks are flushed from sailing," he whispered, tipping his head closer to mine. The corners of his mouth curved upward in the beginnings of a real smile. "Gorgeous."

I grinned, basking in his compliments. It was something I had always wanted him to say, so to hear it made my heart flutter.

"Go on," I murmured as he kissed my neck, just under my ear. His grip on my waist tightened and I tried not to moan at how good he felt. "Don't stop."

"You are so beautiful," he whispered, his words dancing along my skin. "And smart. And funny. Did I mention, wonderful and amazing?"

"Not yet."

"Oh. Well then, you are wonderful and amazing." The smile was apparent in Leo's voice. "I've always thought so."

"Is that so?" I asked, looking up at him.

Leo's blue eyes were serious. The truth shone within them as I dove into his gaze. These weren't just words to get him laid or meant to appease me. These were true. They were what he really felt and thought.

"Yes," he said slowly. "And so much more, Charlotte. There aren't words for how perfect you are to me." He swallowed hard, his blue eyes close to swallowing me whole. "Or how much I love you."

I couldn't breathe. My heart stopped in my chest for an unending moment in time. Leo Westbrook, the man I had loved since the day I first saw him, loved me. Finally.

"I love you, Leo," I whispered back, my voice tight and loose all at the same time.

He kissed me then, slow and sweet, but with so much passion it set my soul aflame.

"Oh, Charlotte..." My name was music when he said it and it made me thrill to the tips of my toes. My whole life, no one ever said my name the way he did. "Stay with me." It wasn't a question or a request, but it wasn't a command either. "Be mine tonight."

I grinned at him. "Why do you think I'm here?"

He pulled me to him, wrapping his arms tighter and breathing in the scent of my hair. His whole body was still, as if he were desperately trying to remember every detail of how I felt in his arms.

"Are you okay?" I asked, hugging him back. "You seem... I don't know... sad. Or disappointed. You sure there isn't something wrong?"

He slowly released his grip on me, letting me go just enough so that I could look up into his beautiful face. The lamp light from his desk cast shadows across his blue eyes and the stubble on his cheeks was longer than it had been this morning, but he still looked perfect to me.

"It's nothing important," he promised. His eyes met mine and for a moment I could see storm clouds behind the beautiful blue of his irises. His fingers tightened across my back. "I need you tonight."

"Then I'm yours." I kissed his lips and whispered, "I've always been yours."

His hands slid into my hair, tangling it between his strong fingers as he kissed me. Without having to think, my hands went around the back of his neck, my pelvis rocking against his as I whimpered into his mouth.

He took his time, kissing me thoroughly. A long, slow swipe of his tongue over my bottom lip, his teeth nibbling the edges of my mouth, his lips pressing against mine. My hand stroked his jaw, feeling the slight prickle of two-day stubble. It wasn't unpleasant, if anything it added to the myriad of wonderful sensations flowing through his kiss. My tongue found his, colliding and tasting. He tasted so good, I knew I could never get enough.

I could have kissed him for hours. Leo knew how to kiss me, knew exactly which way to move and how to open me up to him. But I didn't want to just kiss him. I wanted to make love to him, and if the growing hardness pressed against my lower stomach was any indication, he wanted it too.

I broke away, grinning as I put my hand to his chest. "Mr. Westbrook, I do believe you need to relax. And I happen to know just how to do it."

"Is that so?" One eyebrow cocked upward as the corners of his mouth crept up in an self-assured grin.

I seductively bit my lip, looking him up and down. He had changed from earlier and was now wearing dark slacks with a crisp, light-blue dress shirt. I loved his broad shoulders and slim waist, the way that he managed to look incredibly masculine but without overdoing it.

My fingers went to the top button of his shirt and paused

before undoing the first one. I undid each following, tracing down the line to the button of his pants. He didn't have an undershirt on beneath the dress shirt due to the heat of the Caribbean and I was glad. It meant that his shirt now spilled open and I could see every muscle. All I wanted to do was run my tongue down his abs and taste his skin.

Looking up at him through my eyelashes, I slowly undid his belt buckle and then the zipper to his pants. He stood still, letting me undress his bottom half, even though his breaths were starting to become ragged with want.

With his pants pooled around his ankles, I could see his excitement tenting in his briefs. Somehow, he managed to look even bigger than I recalled from this morning. Even though he wasn't touching me, I felt my skin come alive beneath his gaze.

I tugged his briefs down, releasing his very impressive erection. I took a deep, desired filled breath and let it out slowly before pushing his shoulder. "Have a seat, Mr. Westbrook."

He glanced back behind him, his eyes going to the small leather couch next to the desk. With calm, easy movements, he kicked off his pants and briefs and went to sit. His knees splayed out, revealing his perfect manhood to me.

As seductively as I could, I stepped toward him, swaying my hips and licking my lips. His eyes dilated as I went to my knees before him, tucking myself between his legs. I looked up at him, already wet myself with what I knew I was going to do. I was going to give Leo the most pleasurable night he'd ever had.

I lifted my gaze, making sure his blue eyes were with me as I leaned forward and tasted him. His skin was velvet beneath my lips. He groaned, every muscle tightening as he struggled to stay seated.

"Charlotte," he whispered, lust breaking his voice into a growl. "You don't have to do this."

I raised my chin. "You just need to relax. You've had a long day and need to unwind." With that, I tipped my head back down, running my tongue up his entire length and loving the way he trembled at my touch. He stilled, a deep groan of pleasure vibrating through him.

Spurred on by his reaction and the surprising pleasure I was getting from having him under my control, I swiped my tongue across his broad head, greedily licking and tasting every inch of him. I used my tongue to explore him, to caress his rock hard length. His hips bucked and his hands went to my hair, tangling in it and guiding me to where he wanted.

I let him guide my motions, keeping my mouth and tongue busy on his pleasure as he rocked his hips upward. I could see his washboard abs tighten with every thrust. The muscled V pointing down to his crotch was tight as he clenched it in absolute delight. His rumble of pleasure echoed through the room as I swirled my tongue around him.

"Oh, Charlotte..." I'd never heard his voice so close to breaking as he let his head fall back with ecstasy. The heat between my own thighs intensified as he groaned. "I won't last much longer with you doing that."

If my mouth wasn't so busy, I would have grinned. I loved that I could tip him over the edge so easily. "Let me."

"Not yet. Not, until I've had my turn." He pulled back gently on my hair, pulling my mouth off of him. "Stand up."

Pouting, I didn't stop. I rather liked the idea of getting him off only with the skill of my tongue, but he just tugged a little harder on my hair until I complied. Standing before him, he looked me up and down, lust pouring from his every glance.

"Take the dress off," he commanded, his voice low and powerful. I swallowed once, not sure if I was ready to give in to him. I wanted to go back to my knees and finish what I had started. He stood up, towering over me, eyes dark and powerful. "Take the dress off," he repeated

There was no way I could resist him. I reached for the hem and slowly pulled the sundress up and over my head. His eyes dilated at the sight of my curves still in my swimsuit. He reached out his hand, slowly caressing the curve of my hip. His hand didn't stop there, though. He reached up, untying the back tie of my top. With a quick movement, he had my bra off and on the floor.

He palmed my breast, his big hand caressing my skin. I loved how rough the pads of his fingers were on the sensitive flesh. He leaned forward, tipping his head to take one piqued nipple into his mouth. Teeth softly teased the delicate tissue even tighter and I gasped. My body was aflame with just his touch.

He chuckled as I moaned, arching my back into his face and silently asking for more. "Go lie down," he whispered. "There's more I want to do to you."

I shivered, wondering what beautiful torture he could have planned for me. I stepped back, taking one step before turning to go run to the bed as he had commanded. He caught my arm and grinned, reaching forward and smoothly undoing the side string to the bottom of my bikini.

I stepped forward, the bottoms falling off effortlessly and grinned at him. I loved the way his breath caught as he watched my naked body sashay to the bed where I spread myself out for his delight.

"God, you are so beautiful." He stood at the foot of the

bed and stared for a moment before stripping off his shirt and leaving it laying on the floor. "It isn't fair to make someone as beautiful as you."

I blushed, feeling the heat creep down my bare chest. Leo's compliments always felt more real to me than anyone else's. I looked up at him, naked in the dark of the room. He was so damn handsome and virile that I ached to feel him within me. The need growing between my legs was becoming unbearable.

"Leo," I whimpered. "Don't make me wait."

"Hold onto the headboard," he commanded. I reached up, stretching my body out for his viewing pleasure. I flushed with delight at his sudden intake of breath. His cock jumped, ready to take me right there.

He put one knee on the bed, spreading my legs as he climbed onto the bed. With one knee firmly placed at my groin, he traced the curve of my breast with his fingers. I groaned, arching my hips up as his fingers left magic trails of want across my skin. He pressed his knee higher, giving me something hard to rock against as he touched me. I was already dripping wet with desire, but with his thigh between mine, I started to rock.

His hands came around the undersides of my breasts and cupped them together, creating cleavage. He dipped his head, bringing his lips back to my breasts and kissing them. His stubble rasped against my skin, adding a layer of sensation I wasn't ready for. He played with my nipples, rolling one between his fingers while nipping at the other with his teeth.

I brought my hands down to his head, feeling his hair slide through my fingers as I pressed his face into my chest for more.

"Nuh uh," he said, shaking his head and repeating my phrase from earlier in the day. "Put your hands back up."

I whimpered, but slowly raised them. Once my fingers latched around the headboard, he resumed his gentle touches. I closed my eyes, focusing only on keeping my arms above my head as he showered me with kisses.

"So beautiful," he whispered, caressing each breast with the utmost care and love. His hand slipped down to my stomach, splaying out right before my mound. "So fucking beautiful."

I arched my hips, wanting his fingers to touch me. His thigh was great for rocking against, but I knew his fingers could give me release. He chuckled, the sensual sound filling the room. Slowly, so slowly I was sure I would go insane, he slid his fingers further and further south.

"So wet," he murmured, his fingers teasing with their feather light touch. "So damn perfect..."

The touch of his fingers against my sensitive flesh made it impossible to control the arch of my hips into his hand. A wordless cry of perfect wonder filled my throat as I rode on white lightning into beautiful oblivion at just Leo's touch. I'd never come so easily, and never just at a touch.

It was just what Leo did to me. I was built to respond to his touch without even trying.

Gasping for breath, wordless and lost to wonder, I barely noticed as Leo positioned himself at my entrance. His hands pinned my wrists to the headboard. I bucked my hips, silently begging to be filled with him. I needed him to be a part of me, to physically complete me.

He grit his teeth as he concentrated on going slow. Inch by fantastic inch, he pressed. I couldn't breathe at the sheer amount of pleasure ricocheting through my body. Every part of our bodies that touched singed with lust as he slowly filled me with himself.

He was gentle, concentrating on giving me pleasure. Slow, deep and smooth strokes to fill my every wish. Except, I wanted him. My pleasure would come with his.

"I'm yours, Leo," I whispered, the words falling out without me even having to think. I had always been his. "Take me. Make me yours."

His eyes flashed in the darkness with lust and love. "Oh, Charlotte..." he gasped, ramming the final few inches of himself as deep as he could go. "I don't deserve you..."

"More," I begged. "I want all of you."

He thrust hard and fast, his fingers tight on my wrists, almost to the point of pain as he levered and plunged with reckless abandon. He was filling himself on my body, losing himself to me. My hips and back undulated to his pattern, desperate to keep up with him.

I didn't let go of the headboard. I held on with my knuckles turning white as he filled me again and again. His mouth covered mine, kissing me and pulling me into him.

Every thrust was more powerful than the last. He drove into me with such heat and intensity that I could barely stand it. He was taking me in the most primal fashion I could imagine- using my body to satisfy his own. Pleasure coiled in my stomach, in the tips of my breasts, and seared down my backbone with such intense heat I was sure I was going to light the sheets on fire.

Each thrust brought me higher, brought him higher. I could feel him swell and I cried out, begging for more. I wanted to feel him move within me. I wanted him to bury his unrest in me and to still and let me carry whatever burden he had. I would do anything for Leo. Anything.

His breath came in quick, uneven gasps as his face twisted and grimaced with unbearable pleasure.

I could feel my own body react to his impending climax with one of my own. The way he swelled within me triggered something primal and needy. I contracted down on him, drawing him as deep within me as physically possible and still wanting more. With a wordless, guttural cry, he exploded. Inner muscles I didn't even know I had massaged him deeper, trying to keep him forever within me. I never wanted him to leave me.

The rough, ragged sound of his voice filled my ears like music. My name. My name was on his lips as he lost control of everything. His hips bucked and pushed, even as his cry faded.

Impossible pleasure rocked through me, so deep and pure I couldn't keep my eyes open. Every muscle clenched and relaxed, shaking and trembling with unadulterated pleasure. I'd never experienced anything so powerful. This was what it meant for two people to come together. This was what sex was supposed to be. A meeting and merging and pleasure so strong that it defied logic.

"I love you, Charlotte," Leo gasped. He loosened his grip on my wrists, massaging them gently with his fingers. His eyes were dark pools that I wanted to swim in forever. I could see forever in his eyes and it was beautiful.

"I love you, Leo," I whispered back, meaning it with every ounce of my being.

He leaned forward and kissed me and I knew that this was where I was always meant to be.

19

___

The room was full of sunlight, but empty of Leo.

My hand felt for him on his side of the bed before I opened my eyes, but I knew he was gone before ever stretching out my hand.

I sighed. When I slept with him, I didn't get the nightmares of being alone, but waking up by myself was almost as bad. I hated being alone more than anything.

With a groan, I rolled out of bed and opened a drawer to find something to wear. A pair of boxers and a clean white t-shirt that smelled like Leo were perfect pajamas.

I picked up my phone to check my schedule and found twelve new emails. I had work to do today, even though I really just wanted to take another day off.

Screw it, I thought setting the phone back down on the nightstand, *I'm going back to bed. Maybe I'll go back to sleep and when I wake up Leo will be here.*

It sounded like a solid plan. Avoidance and procrastination were always the best solutions in regards to work. Sometimes.

I had just snuggled back under the covers, tucking my head under the pillow, when the bedroom door opened.

"Good morning, beautiful," Leo said, his voice warm and smooth like honey. That was the greeting I had been wanting earlier. It made waking up worth it. I popped my head out from under it's downy castle and saw that Leo had a tray. A tray with coffee and food. Leo grinned. "Breakfast awaits, madam."

I moved the pillow behind me and scooted up in bed as Leo placed the tray over my lap. The smell of pancakes and bacon was overwhelming and my mouth started to water. He even had my coffee with two creams and sugars.

"You didn't have to do this," I said, noticing that the tray came complete with a small vase holding a tropical flower. A happy warmth surged behind my breastbone.

"I know." Leo shrugged, sitting on the edge of the bed and watching my reaction with a smile. "I wanted to."

I grinned at him. No one had ever made me breakfast in bed. Ever. Not even Bastian. But it was something I had always wanted to experience. The idea of someone taking the time to prepare me food, and then bring it to me without having to be asked, or without me even having to crawl out of bed, was one of utter care. Only special people got breakfast in bed. Of course it would be Leo who would give that experience to me. There was a very good reason why I was in love with him.

"Are you going to eat?" I asked, pouring the pitcher of syrup all over the pancakes and letting it dribble onto the bacon. It was thick and heavy and I knew it had to be real maple syrup and not the knock off kind. Leo really was the best.

"I already ate. I woke up early," he said with a shrug. "I couldn't sleep so I went for a run."

I was too busy stuffing a bite of pancakes into my mouth to ask why he couldn't sleep. I had slept like the dead.

"So, I was thinking..." Leo ran his fingers through his hair, making it stand on end.

"Uh oh." I dropped my fork. "That's not what a girl ever wants to hear after her boyfriend has done something nice."

"This has nothing to do with that." Leo chuckled, moving to sit beside me. He swiped a piece of bacon off my plate. "I think we should tell your brother about us."

"I didn't know you had a death wish," I replied with a grin. Inside, I was doing cartwheels. We were going to go public. Everyone would know. He could kiss me in front of Toby and it wouldn't matter. We could hold hands. We could go out on dates without having to sneak out of the house. It would be fantastic... if he survived my brother.

"You're worth it. Besides, I think it's time." Leo ruffled his hair again. "I timed myself on my run this morning, and I'm pretty sure I'm faster than him."

I giggled. "And you have Murdoch. I'm pretty sure Murdoch could take Eli, but if it's Bastian and Eli, you're screwed."

"Wow. You're filling me with confidence." He rolled his eyes.

I fiddled with my breakfast for a moment. "You remember what he did to my first boyfriend?"

"The one he caught coming out of your college dorm room at six am?" Leo let out a low whistle as he remembered. "He did not look good with a broken nose. Though, I wanted to beat the guy to a pulp, too. That smug smile still makes me want to hit him."

A warmth filled me. Even then, Leo had liked me.

"Yeah, well thanks to Bastian, that guy never called me

again." I shook my head. Bastian could be very scary when he wanted to be. Especially when it came to his little sister. I frowned. "If Bastian beats you up, you'll still call me, right?"

Leo planted a kiss on my forehead. "As long as you come see me in the hospital."

I laughed, but it was more of a nervous titter than humorous guffaw. I wasn't sure what Bastian was going to do. Leo was his friend, but I was his little sister. He'd scared off more guys than I could count and he wasn't afraid to lose his temper. I loved that he wanted to keep me safe, but at the same time, I was a full-grown woman now.

I hoped Bastian would be okay with Leo.

"We'll break it to him easy," I said. "In a public place. With Ava." I paused. "I bet she'd even be willing to tie him down for us."

"I don't want to think about Ava tying Bastian down, thanks." Leo stuck his tongue out at me and I giggled. "But, you're right. Some place public, with Ava there, and preferably when he's in a good mood."

"Oh, so like... never." I sighed.

"Tonight." Leo kissed my forehead again. "We'll tell him tonight."

"Okay." A delightful pressure was growing behind my breastbone. I loved this man. He was willing to face the wrath of my brother for me. It was going to be scary. But, he was going to do it for me.

We had a plan.

Without warning, the bedroom door opened. I turned, expecting it to be the housekeeper or maybe Murdoch. Instead, to my absolute mortification, in walked Bastian and Gabe.

I tried to pull the sheet up a little higher, but the breakfast tray made it a little hard to do. I was incredibly glad I had decided to put on some clothing, but even so, having my brother walk in on me in Leo's bed wearing Leo's t-shirt, wasn't exactly the way I had planned on informing my brother that Leo and I were a couple.

This was not the plan.

"Hey, Charlotte," Gabe greeted me, walking in and leaning against the far wall without a care in the world. I stared at him, clutching the sheet like a shield. I could feel my blush searing down my skin and was half afraid I was going to light the bed on fire I was blushing so hot.

"Hi, Charlotte," Bastian echoed, coming in and sitting down on the foot of the bed like everything was completely normal. "Sorry to interrupt, but we just got good news."

I stared at my brother sitting calmly on the edge of the bed while I sat there with sex sleep hair.

I couldn't be more mortified if I tried.

"The phone application is basically user ready," Gabe gushed excitedly. "The beta group loves it. Leo, you and Charlotte did a fantastic job."

"Charlotte gets most of the credit," Leo said quickly. Somehow he wasn't bright red, but he was carefully putting distance between himself and Bastian. "She's the one who made me keep working at it until it was perfect."

Bastian and Gabe continued to talk about the app as I looked back and forth between them all and Leo's jaw hung open. He stared openly at Bastian, his head cocked to the side as if he wasn't sure this was real.

To be honest, I wasn't sure the man sitting by my feet *was* my brother. My brother should be growling and holding Leo against the wall with a fist cocked back while Gabe tried to hold him back. He should be defending my honor while I screamed at him to let me live my life. That was how it was supposed go- how it had always gone. He wasn't supposed to be sitting there like this was the most normal thing in the world.

No one had said anything yet about the fact that I was sleeping in Leo's bed. Everyone was behaving as if this were the most normal thing. I had no idea why Bastian wasn't screaming death threats. The scar over his eye wasn't even twitching.

The only reasonable explanation was that Bastian had been abducted by aliens. Or this was a dream and the smell of pancakes was just really vivid.

"So, dinner tonight to celebrate," Gabe said. "Adele's Restaurant, since she makes the best food on the island other than Leo."

The other two boys murmured their assent and somehow my head moved in approval as well. I just kept tugging at the sheet, hoping I wouldn't knock my tray of pancakes over in my attempt to disappear.

Gabe pushed off the wall and went to the bedroom door. "Great. See you all at six." Gabe grinned at everyone. "Looking great, by the way, Charlotte."

He left the door open, whistling as he went down the hall. I hid a little more under the blanket.

But Bastian didn't do anything.

"Enjoy your morning off, but remember I have work for you this afternoon." Bastian patted my leg through the bedspread before standing and heading to the door himself. "See you later, Leo."

And with that, my brother, who should have been pissed that his little sister was in someone's bed, walked out of the room with a smile on his face.

The room was empty for three whole minutes before I regained the ability to speak.

"What the hell just happened?" I asked, staring at the door and feeling like I'd just survived a hurricane. I looked over at Leo.

"The app's going live. It's a good thing." He shrugged.

I chucked the pillow at his head. The damn phone app was the last thing I was worried about. "Not the app! Them!" I waved my arms at the door where Bastian and Gabe had just disappeared. "No offense, but how do you not have a black eye right now? I'm in your bed! The guy who took me to prom got a black eye and being in your bed is far worse than a crappy corsage!"

"To be fair, that guy was a jerk," Leo replied with a shrug. "I'm not a jerk."

I grabbed another pillow and chucked it at him again. He easily caught it and laughed.

"I have no idea what just happened," Leo said, looking at the door like it led to another world. "But, apparently, Bastian's good with us being together and I'm still alive. So, I'm not going to complain."

The door knocked and I turned to stare at it, worried at what other craziness might walk through that door.

It was just Bastian.

"Did I leave my phone in here?" he asked, poking his head in. He then came into room and went to the foot of the bed, walking as nonchalantly as a cat. "Ah, here it is. Must have fell out of my pocket."

Bastian grinned at me as I stared at him, my jaw on my chest. There was no way this was really happening. No way.

Bastian picked up his phone and went back to the door like nothing about this scenario was strange.

"That's it?" I squeaked, still clutching the sheet.

Bastian paused at the doorway, finally taking pity on me.

He grinned like this was the funniest thing in the whole world. To him, it probably was.

"Charlotte, thank god you finally got together. It was painful to watch you two dance around each other for this long." His grin melted into an angry face. The scar pulsed white. "But, Leo- you hurt her and I swear to God, you are a dead man. Understand?"

"Yes." Leo took a protective step toward me. Bastian's eyes darkened at the insinuation that he would do such a thing. "You know that'll never happen. I'd never hurt her." Bastian looked ready to punch Leo's lights out. "I love her."

My heart melted completely.

The scary gleam vanished from Bastian's eyes. "I know. That's why your face is still intact right now." Bastian grinned. "Also, do you know where Murdoch is? He owes me twenty bucks."

"Kitchen," Leo answered, frowning slightly. "He seems to owe a lot of people money this week."

"Thanks." Bastian winked at me. "See you later."

I could hear him chuckling as he walked down the hallway.

"I'm in the Twilight Zone," I said to Leo. "Somewhere, someone is narrating my life with a weird twist ending."

Leo plopped onto the foot of the bed, staring at the doorway again. "I guess we aren't nearly as secretive as we thought."

"Did everyone but the two of us know this was going to happen? No one seems even remotely surprised." I stabbed my eggs with a fork. "Wish they would've shared that with me."

Leo chuckled and put his hand on mine. "I don't know... I think things worked out pretty well."

I looked up from my breakfast into his kind, blue eyes.

The sun shone on his hair and there was a sparkle in his eyes that made my chest fill up with longing and joy.

"You're right," I said softly, smiling as I looked at the man I loved. This was perfect and if it had happened any other way, I wasn't sure it would feel this good. "I wouldn't change this for the world."

20

It had been a good morning. A very good morning.

I grinned as I approached the mansion, humming to myself and feeling good about the world and everything in it. Leo and I were officially a couple and my brother was okay with it. Things were finally going the way I had always imagined.

A security guard waved as I approached, recognizing me and opening up the main gate. I walked in, shaking my head at the massive house in front of me.

Soon, this mansion wouldn't be ours anymore. It had been sold as part of the auction, and in a few weeks, all of the furniture would be gone and we'd be back in New York. I was actually okay with selling it. I loved the location of the mansion, as well as the view, but the building was far too big and gaudy. It screamed wealth and money and that was the last thing I cared about.

I much preferred the idea of a cute little two bedroom bungalow on the beach to the massive monstrosity full of old artwork and antique furniture designed to impress. I liked comfort more.

I stepped inside and nearly tripped over a pair of sandals. They weren't the right size or style for Bastian, but were most definitely men's sandals. And there was a pair of women's flip-flops alongside the door. I stared at them for a moment before remembering that Ava's father and his girl-friend arrived yesterday.

I knew I'd have to say hello to them later, but for now, I needed to get to work. Despite being in the Caribbean, there were things that needed to be done. Billions of dollars didn't just keep track of themselves.

I ran up to my room and changed into some light cotton slacks and a silk blouse. Even though I'd be working from home today, I wanted to look professional. Besides, if I was dressed for work, I wouldn't be tempted to leave because I'd have to change.

I knocked on Bastian's office door before going in to check with him what he needed for the day. He was sitting at his desk while Ava lounged on the couch next to him with a book. Both of them looked like cats that had found the cream.

"What's up, boss?" I asked, pulling out my tablet. I still had some things that needed to be done with the phone app, but Bastian's news this morning that the beta testers loved it was incredibly encouraging.

"Those reports you asked for are in," Bastian replied. "I also need you to schedule a press release."

I looked up from my tablet. "A press release? For what?"

Bastian looked over at Ava and grinned. He looked happier than I'd ever seen him. "Ava, you want to tell her?"

Ava jumped up from the couch and hurried over to me, holding out her left hand. A big, shiny rock glittered on her left ring finger. "We're engaged!"

I let out an inhumanely high, excited *SQUEE!!!!* and

began jumping up and down while trying to hug her. "I get a sister! I'm so excited for you two!"

Ava laughed, hugging me back and jumping with me. "It won't be for a while. We want a longer engagement, but..." She looked over at Bastian and grinned.

"But there just wasn't a good reason to wait to ask," Bastian finished. He smiled back at her and I could feel the love in the room.

"That's why you had me fly Ava's dad out, isn't?" I asked, finally stopping my jumping. "So you could ask him permission?"

"I felt it was something I should do in person." Bastian paused, his smile faltering. "I'm sorry I didn't tell you earlier. I figured when you said that I should marry Ava, that you were serious and-"

"-and you were right," I cut him off. I let go of Ava and ran over to hug my brother. He held me tight and I could feel the happiness radiating off him in waves. "I'm so happy for you, Bastian. So. Happy."

He released me, and I realized he had picked me up off the floor in his bear hug. "Thank you," he said with a bashful grin. His eyes flashed over to Ava and his smile softened into something that melted my heart. He walked around his desk and put his arm over Ava's shoulder. She instinctively leaned into him and smiled.

"You two are just too damn cute," I groaned, rolling my eyes. "So lovey-dovey."

Actually, I love it, I thought to myself. This was a true romance story. This was what love looked like and I couldn't be gladder that my brother had it. If anyone deserved happiness, it was him.

"Like you aren't exactly the same," Ava teased. She

grinned at my confused expression. "I heard you were in Leo's bed this morning."

Red heat flushed through my entire body and I suddenly felt a little dizzy with the sudden loss of blood to the full body blush.

"And to think I had to hear it from this guy," Ava continued, mock hurt filling her voice. She pouted her lips out. "I thought we were friends, Charlotte."

"Um..." I couldn't find words. "Well..."

"I told you it would work out!" Ava grinned at me, holding onto Bastian. "I knew it from the moment I saw the two of you together."

I looked back and forth between their knowing grins and sighed. "I'm so glad everyone is so involved in my love life."

Bastian laughed. "It just means we care."

I rolled my eyes at him. "You said those reports were in?" I asked, changing the subject.

"Yup." He grinned, knowing exactly what I was doing to change the subject.

"Then I need to get to work." I went to hug Ava. "I'm so happy for you. I couldn't ask for a better sister."

"Thanks," she whispered back, giving me one last squeeze before letting me go.

I turned and headed out of Bastian's office, glancing back as I closed the door behind me to see the two of them looking deeply into one another's eyes. If love was a visible color, the room would have been saturated in it.

I grinned, closing the door and heading to my own office. Today was a good day.

21

"You ready to go?" Bastian asked, popping his head into my office.

I looked up in surprise. I had been so focused on my work that I had completely lost track of time.

"Um..." I looked at my almost complete report. With the gala and auction, I was behind on keeping track of all the financials for Bastian. "I just need to finish this and hit save. You go on ahead. I'll be right there."

"Okay," Bastian agreed. "See you in a bit."

I could hear him talking to Ava in the hall. Another male voice that I assumed was Mr. Fairchild asked him a question, but by then they were too far down the hall for me to make out what was said. The front door opened and closed as Bastian, Ava, and Ava's parents left for the restaurant.

It only took me a couple of moments to finish entering the last bit of data and to press save. Somehow, these reports always seemed to get longer the more I had to do. I reached for the lid on my laptop just as a notification for an email came in. I thought about just ignoring it, but it was from the financial department and was probably important.

With a sigh, I opened it. The content just made me sigh again.

Apparently, money was missing from the CEO slush fund. The account was supposed to be for emergency business transactions, and it was closely monitored by the accountants. About one hundred thousand dollars was unaccounted for. I groaned, not wanting to deal with this right now. My stomach was rumbling for some food, so I just put an important label on the email for later.

The accountants were always on me for this account, never the billionaires. It wasn't quite fair, but I dealt with it. I knew it was important to keep all our numbers accurate. It was probably just a forgotten private jet flight or some dinner expense that Gabe, Leo, or Bastian forgot to mark down. Since they were the only ones other than me with access to that account, I knew it was just a mistake somewhere.

If it wasn't, there would be hell to pay.

I closed my laptop and hurried upstairs to put on something more appropriate for a night out in the Caribbean with friends. I put on a light pink sundress with a pretty floral pattern that was breezy and comfortable while still chic and classy.

Outside, it was humid and hot, especially after the cool of the air conditioner. A Porsche with a driver was waiting for me in front of the mansion, the air conditioning already going and the seats cool. I was glad I wasn't driving. Despite having access to cars that would make most people drool, I hated driving them. I really preferred my old beat up truck back home to these finicky little sports cars.

The drive was short and pleasant. The driver pulled up to the main entrance and stopped the car, running out to open my door for me. The heat of the island hit me, somehow warmer here than it was back at the mansion.

I thanked him and he drove off, heading back to the mansion and revving the engine slightly. I hoped he enjoyed driving the car. Someone should. I laughed quietly as I heard the engine again further up the road. It was the perfect day for driving a fast car. The skies were clear and the roads open. The driver was having a little fun and I was glad.

I went to open the door when I saw Leo coming up from the beach walk with Robbie and Sam. My brow creased, thinking that he should be coming from the opposite direction than they were. Which meant that they were probably coming from the docks. Where that stupid speedboat was.

I hoped Leo was keeping his promise not to drive it.

"As much as I hate to say it, that racing boat of yours is a modern marvel," Robbie's voice drifted up as they approached. My heart sunk a little bit, hearing his words. "Thanks for letting me look at it."

"Any time," Leo replied. "I won't be taking it out any time soon. However, I just found a new driver who is interested. That boat could be going for the record."

I sighed a little in relief. He wasn't out on that death trap boat. I felt bad for even thinking he was.

"Hey, Charlotte," Leo greeted me, a smile filling his face as they came up on the deck. Robbie and Sam exchanged knowing looks and darted inside.

He paused for a moment, glancing about before remembering that everyone already knew about us and kissed me. Kissed me good enough that if I had been wearing socks, they would have been knocked off.

It felt freeing to kiss him, knowing that everyone already knew and supported us.

"Wow," I said, breathless from his kiss. That man knew how to use his lips in the best possible way. The kiss was short and sweet, but it still made me swoon. We were officially a couple now, especially if we were kissing in front of restaurants.

"Blech. Some of us would like to eat," Gabe said, gently pushing past us to get to the door. "Seriously, get a room."

I laughed, scooting closer to Leo to let Gabe pass. Gabe held the door, giving me a wink as we passed. I knew he was happy for us, even if he had to tease.

Inside, it was cool and dark. The hostess showed us to the back party room where Sam and Robbie had already joined Ava, Bastian, and Ava's father and girlfriend. Sam waved, pulling her chair up to the table and chastising Robbie for not using a napkin.

It was a small room, but it had a large window that looked out over the ocean view. Flutes of champagne were already out on the table.

"It looks like everyone's here," Gabe remarked, picking up a glass of champagne from the table. He tapped on it to quiet the room. "Thank you all for coming. If you will join me, let us toast to Kindling Dating's newest mobile app."

Gabe raised his glass, his eyes going over all the happy couples. Watching him take in Bastian and Ava, then Robbie and Sam, Ava's father and his date, and then Leo and I, I realized that Gabe was the odd man out. He didn't have a date. As official fairy godmother to Ava and Bastian, I was eventually going to have to remedy this.

Gabe cleared his throat, raising his glass a little higher. "Good things are coming. Cheers."

Everyone echoed the sentiment and took a sip of champagne.

The room settled into quiet conversation. Ava and

Bastian were talking animatedly with Robbie while Sam laughed at something said by Ava's father. I sipped on my champagne, leaning comfortably against Leo.

Leo wrapped his arm around my waist and rested his head on mine as we stood there, just watching the people we cared most about in the world smile and laugh over the success of the business. The phone app was going to be huge for us. The business was booming and it was all because three knuckle-headed boys found a loan and gave their idea a go.

A loud buzzing rumbled in Leo's pants pocket. He frowned, letting me go to check it. His face darkened as he hit the reject button and he stuffed it back into his pocket. He barely let it go before it began to go off again.

"Damn it," he whispered, smashing the buttons harder this time. Something that almost looked like fear shifted across his eyes, but was gone before I could really tell. He ran his fingers through his hair. It was an unconscious gesture he only did when he was nervous.

"Everything okay?" I asked, noting the sudden tension in his shoulders.

"It's fine," he said sharply. He smiled, taking the sting out of his tone, even if it wasn't a real smile. "It's just Toby." He pointed to his phone, the notification light going crazy. "I need to take this. You stay here and enjoy the party."

"Okay..." I cocked my head to the side, confused. Something wasn't right. After seeing them at the meeting together, I wondered if Toby was having trouble with gambling again. Leo kissed my cheek and hurried out the door to find a silent place to take his call.

I watched him, only checking out his ass a little, as he disappeared. His strides were long and hurried, and there was a tension in his shoulders I had never seen before.

There was something wrong, something that he wasn't telling me, but I wasn't sure what.

I bit my lip, wishing I could help him. He didn't have to keep things from me anymore. We were a couple now. I could help him if he would just let me.

"I'm glad you two finally got together," Gabe said, grabbing my attention. He moved to stand next to me, sipping on his champagne. "It's good to see you both so happy."

"Thanks," I replied. "Now we just need to get you someone."

Gabe laughed. "No, thank you. Someone has to be the designated bachelor. We run a dating company after all. Can't have us all falling in love. Especially if it's not through our services."

"If you change your mind, let me know." I grinned at him. "I love a good love story, especially when it involves billionaires."

"Don't we all," he remarked, taking a sip of his drink. Something in the way he twisted his mouth and gulped at the liquid made me pause. There was far too much emotion in the movement.

"You met someone, didn't you?" I guessed.

"What?" Gabe nearly spit out his drink.

"You met someone, didn't you?" I repeated, wondering who could have captured Gabe's heart. He was always flirting with some sweet young thing or another, but they never seemed to last long. He loved his flavors of the month, but never had anyone that made him sad when they left.

Gabe stared at his half-empty champagne flute for a moment, as if seeking the answer in the clear golden liquid. "Can't keep anything from you, can I, Miss Nosy-pants?" He sighed and shrugged. "I thought I did. She was... there was a connection that I haven't felt before."

"What happened?" I asked softly.

He looked over, his face twisting into a sad grin that only made the loneliness in his usually joyful eyes even more obvious. "Apparently, she feels differently." He tilted up his glass and finished the last of his drink in one long gulp.

I put my hand on his arm. "I'm sorry, Gabe." I hated to see him like this. Even though he was much more my brother's friend than mine, I had grown up with him and his little sister. I gave his arm a gentle squeeze. "Well, I hope you're not pining away for me."

If he had been drinking, he would have most certainly done a real spit take.

"You?" Disgust dripped from his voice at the notion. "That's revolting!"

"Wow," I said, taking back my hand and holding it like he had hurt me. "Thank you for boosting my self esteem."

Gabe shook his head, trying to take back his harsh words. "No, it's just..." He paused as he realized I was grinning at him.

"Don't worry, I find you revolting as well," I assured him.

"You're not revolting," he amended. "It's just, when I look at you, I don't see a hot, sexy woman. I see a little girl in pigtails playing tea party with Chloe. I can't *not* see that."

I smiled, remembering hundreds of afternoons playing princess with Gabe's little sister while the two older boys ran around outside in the backyard. We'd try to get them to join in on our games, but they both thought we were just stupid girls.

"I can't see you as anything but my sister," he trailed off and made a face. "So, sorry, but *blech*."

I laughed. To be honest, the idea of kissing Gabe was about as disgusting as the idea of kissing Bastian. I'd rather eat dinner off my shoes after walking through a public park.

"You're killing all my hopes and dreams of us, Gabey-poo," I teased, pushing out my bottom lip in the biggest fake pout I could manage.

Gabe rolled his eyes. "You're *sooooooo* funny."

I laughed, dropping the pout. "I am pretty hilarious, thanks."

"I'm happy for you and Leo, though," Gabe said, smiling as he looked down at me. "It's been a long time coming."

"People keep saying that," I replied, shaking my head. "Don't tell me- Murdoch owes you twenty bucks, too?"

"Nope." Gabe shook his head and grinned. "He owes me forty."

"Poor Murdoch's going to go broke!" I laughed. "He can't keep betting all you billionaires on a bodyguard salary."

"That's probably why he hasn't made any other bets with us," Gabe observed. He looked around the room and then down at his watch. "Speaking of Leo's personal protection, where is Leo? Bastian looks like he might explode if he doesn't make a toast about his engagement soon."

Bastian and Ava were practically bouncing with excitement. Sam was oohing and ahhing over her ring.

"I'll go find him," I offered, handing Gabe my empty champagne flute. "Let Bastian make the announcement without me if necessary."

"Will do," Gabe said. He grinned and I turned to hurry out of the restaurant to go find Leo.

22

I took a deep breath, inhaling the scent of ocean, hot sand, growing trees, and the scent of Adele's amazing food. Other than Leo's cologne, it was possibly my favorite scent in the world. Outside the sun was just touching the horizon, turning the ocean into melted gold while the sky bruised purple in the distance. The crickets and frogs were already starting their nightly chorus, tuning their cries like an orchestra before a concert. I loved this place, this island so much.

Leo wasn't on the porch, but I figured he had to be nearby. The bar to the right was slowly gaining patrons, so I knew he wasn't that direction. There was a small touristy gift shop to the left, but they were closed. I peeked inside, thinking of how I should get one of the conch shells and send it to Chloe.

The sound of Leo's voice caught my attention. I followed it around the corner to the side of the building. It was a quiet spot where no one would bother him, so it made sense for him to have gone there. I couldn't see him yet, just hear his voice.

"I've done everything you've asked," Leo growled into his phone. I paused before he could see me, not wanting to interrupt what was apparently a heated phone conversation. "It's time for you to hold up your end of the bargain."

I knew I should back up and not listen to what he was saying, that it was a private conversation, yet my feet didn't move.

"I gave you the money, all one hundred fucking grand of it," Leo roared. He quieted as the person on the other line spoke. "No, no... I don't want her to know that. I don't want anyone to know that. Why do you think I've been giving in to your demands?"

My hand went to my mouth. I could only think of one 'her' he could be talking about. Me. What didn't he want me to know and who was he paying?

"Fine. Another hundred grand." Leo's voice was hard and unkind. "Then I'm done. This never gets out."

Blackmail. That's what was going on here. There was something that Leo didn't want me to know and he was willing to pay off whoever it was that knew. One hundred thousand dollars. Something about the figure stuck in my brain.

The CEO slush fund.

But that didn't make sense. Leo was a billionaire. There was no reason for him not to just pay it out of his own bank account. There was no reason to use the corporate slush fund that was tracked and followed by accountants, unless...

Unless he was gambling again. Unless he didn't have access to his bank accounts. If he was gambling and needed quick cash, the CEO slush fund would look like the perfect place to get some money.

Oh, Leo. What are you doing? I pressed my hand harder

against my mouth. He said he hadn't gambled since college, but what if he was? What if that was why Toby was at the meeting last night? It explained so much, even though it left a horrible sinking feeling in the pit of my stomach.

Anger seared up and out of that dark pit in my stomach. How could he do this to us? Things were just getting to be perfect. We were finally together and happy. Our friends were happy and the business was due to make another few billion dollars with this new app. Why now?

I stomped around the corner of the building, anger making me brave and stupid.

"Leo!" I growled.

He spun around startled, nearly dropping his phone in the process. "Charlotte! What are you doing here?"

I stalked up to him, furious that I only came up to his chest. I wished I was tall enough to glare down at him like an angry parent. "I came to get you. There's a party inside. A party of your *friends*."

Friends you are lying to. Friends like me, I thought.

"I'll be right in," Leo replied, confused at the anger in my voice. "I just needed to make another call first."

I crossed my arms, not moving. I wasn't about to leave to let him to transfer more money out of the slush fund. "Did you take the slush fund money, Leo?"

"Slush fund money?" Leo sounded genuinely confused, but I wasn't born yesterday. "What are you talking about?"

"There's money missing from the slush fund. One hundred thousand dollars." I pressed my lips together, trying to keep my voice even. "I didn't know where it went, until I find you back here talking about giving people hundred's of thousands of dollars. What are you doing Leo?"

Leo's eyes flashed with darkness. "That's none of your business."

"Leo, if you're gambling..." I took a step forward, uncrossing my arms and holding out my hands to him. "Please let me help you."

"You think I'm gambling?" Hurt and betrayal filled Leo's face. He stepped back as if I had punched him in the gut.

"Leo, it's okay." I took another step forward.

His face twisted and he shook his head, anger filling his eyes. "How dare you?"

"I'm just trying to help. I love you, Leo, and I don't want anything bad to happen to you," I said. Stealing money from the company slush fund was a big deal. I wasn't sure how forgiving Bastian and Gabe would be, but I was determined to help him.

"I don't need your help, Charlotte." He spat out my name like it left a bad taste in his mouth. "I've got everything under control."

He straightened to his full height and tugged his shirt smooth before pushing past me to get back to the restaurant. I took a step back, surprised at how uncaring his attitude was. I was just trying to help him, but here he was acting like I was the enemy.

"Right," I sneered, hating how catty I sounded even in my own head but unable to stop. "Because that phone call sounded very in control."

Leo froze, every muscle in his back going stiff. He turned slowly. "It's none of your business, Charlotte." His eyes narrowed and his voice was low and dangerous. "You need to drop it."

"It *is* my business, Leo," I snapped. How dare he put me in this position? The money was missing from the slush fund in the exact amount he was paying his blackmailer. It wasn't rocket science to figure out they were related and it certainly wasn't legal. "It's personal, professional and every thing in between. It is entirely my business."

"Let it go, Charlotte." Leo's eyes flashed. "It isn't what you think it is."

"I just want to help-"

"I don't need your help!" Leo roared. His lips curled back in a snarl and the vein on his neck pumped with angry heartbeats. "I don't *want* your help."

"Leo, if you're gambling..."

"I'm not gambling!" His whole body was tense and vibrating with anger. "I can't believe this. I tell you my biggest shame and you throw it in my face. You have no right, no right at all, sticking your nose into my business. This isn't your problem."

"What the hell, Leo?" I hated the way I knew my face was flushing and how much I was shaking. I hated that we were fighting and I hated the way he was looking at me. There was betrayal and seething anger in his every glance.

"I don't need this." Leo turned and started walking away from the restaurant.

"Leo, don't make me get Bastian." I grabbed his arm, and as he looked down at me I knew it was the wrong thing to do. I should have just let him go off and cool down, but no. Now he was really mad. Now I had crossed the line.

He shook off my hands as if I were nothing. His eyes went up and down my body once, but there was no joy or even lust in the look. "If that's what you're going to do, then I guess I don't need you."

I don't need you. His words hit me like a Mac truck.

"Leo..."

"I never should have let anyone know how I feel about

you. This was a mistake," he hissed, turning and walking away. "Stay away from me, Charlotte."

I stared after him, unable to move, unable to speak as he disappeared into the darkening sunset.

A mistake. I don't need you.

What had just happened?

"Hey, Charlotte."

Bastian's voice was low and soothing, but I didn't pick my head up off the bar. I didn't move. I just stayed there, my face pressed against the plastic that smelled like beer and wished I could curl up and die.

"What are you doing here?" he asked. I could feel his presence now on the bar-stool beside me and I peeked open one eye to see him smiling kindly at me. I wished he would just go back next door and leave me alone to cry.

"Being miserable." I turned my head to face the other direction, but still on the bar. "Go away, Bastian. I want to mope."

He moved seats so I had to look at him again. "Can I mope, too?"

I groaned and pulled myself off the bar. I knew him well enough to know he wasn't going to leave me alone. "Where's Ava? Shouldn't you two be dancing off into the sunset or something?"

"She's convincing Robbie to take her sailing tomorrow and to let her steer." He chuckled and shook his head fondly before focusing on me again. "What are you doing getting drunk? On a workday?"

"I'm not drunk. I've only had one drink." I looked at the single empty shot glass of rum on the counter. I wanted about thirty-seven more. Maybe then my heart wouldn't hurt so much. "I wanted to get drunk, but the hangover tomorrow sounded miserable."

Bastian raised his eyebrows and crossed his arms, clearly not believing I was that sensible. "Right. A hangover."

"Fine. I forgot my wallet. The bartender is new and wont give me credit." I slumped forward and played with the empty glass as Bastian laughed. I glared at him. "I'm glad you think it's funny."

"A little," Bastian said with one last chuckle. "And that was a nice attempt at getting me off track. Why are you here, Charlotte?"

I sighed. "Leo and I had a fight."

Bastian frowned, obviously confused. "About what?"

"I overheard something..." I didn't want to tell him about the phone conversation or the money missing from the slush fund. Not yet. I couldn't do that to Leo, not until he had the chance to make it right. I couldn't do it to him. "I don't know. Just a fight."

Bastian stood up and put his hands on my shoulders. It felt like the weight of the world.

"You know Leo. He's hot-headed," Bastian said. "He'll go do something to cool down and he'll apologize tomorrow. Just like he always does when he does something stupid. Things will work out just fine."

I flipped the shot glass upside down, wishing I had another. "I hope so."

Except we'd never had a fight like this. I'd never seen Leo with eyes so angry. I'd never pushed him that hard. I'd never had him look at me like that. His eyes and whatever terrible emotion that I was trying to avoid identifying was going to haunt me forever. This wasn't a normal fight.

"I know so," Bastian told me, his voice full of confidence I didn't share. "Come on. You need food."

"Restaurant's closed now," I informed him, even though he had to know since he had just come from there.

"How about a Rough Day Sandwich?" he offered.

"Yes, please." It wasn't going to fix my problems, but Bastian's Rough Day Sandwiches were good for the soul.

"Okay." Bastian gave my shoulders one last squeeze before letting go. "Let's go rescue Robbie from Ava and we'll head home."

I nodded, slowly sliding from the bar stool. As I followed Bastian out of the bar, I looked down at the path Leo had taken, wishing that we had never had this stupid fight.

I hoped Bastian was right. I hoped that Leo was just off cooling down and that we'd be right as rain in the morning.

I hoped. But I wasn't going to hold my breath.

24

———

I couldn't sleep.

The clock said I had been trying to sleep for the past three hours, but it felt more like an eternity. Bastian's sandwich lay heavy in my stomach since it was too knotted up with fear and heartbreak to actually digest any food.

I kicked off my comforter and was immediately too cold. But it was too hot to sleep with it on. With a sigh, I got up and went to the thermostat for the fourth time tonight. I couldn't find the right temperature and I had a feeling it was more to do with me than the thermostat.

I was hot with anger and cold with shame.

Giving up on the thermostat, I put on a pair of shorts and a t-shirt. Maybe a walk on the beach would put me in a better mood. The ocean was usually magic for heartbroken lovers, right?

Yeah, to drown their sorrows, I answered myself bitterly. Still, walking the beach sounded like a better idea than tossing and turning in bed for another five hours.

The house was silent as I crept to the back door and

escaped out onto the porch. The night air was hot after the air-conditioned house and far more humid, but the breeze off the ocean was pleasant. The crickets were almost deafening at this hour. I hoped they were having better luck with their mates than I was.

I paused at the steps down to the beach, my hand on the railing. This is where Leo kissed me. This porch. Two steps to the left.

I closed my eyes and replayed our fight for the millionth time, trying to figure out how I could fix it. But the truth was, I couldn't. I couldn't fix this. Not without Leo's help. I'd hurt him. Even if he was gambling, I shouldn't have accused him without being sure. I could only imagine how it must have felt to have his biggest secret thrown back in his face at the first hint of trouble, yet I knew he was still hiding something from me.

That wasn't why he told me about it. He had trusted me. And by accusing him, I had betrayed that trust. There were other reasons the money could be missing from the slush account. Maybe it really was just coincidence that he was being blackmailed for that amount. Maybe Gabe had taken a model out on a jet trip and forgotten to expense report it right away.

"He'll go do something to calm down..." Bastian's words echoed in my mind as I looked out at the water. The moon was barely a sliver of light on the dark water.

I knew what Leo would want to do to cool down. Drive that stupid boat of his. To go fast, skimming over the water and letting his troubles fade while he risked just a little more speed.

Except he promised.

Except we had argued.

He had said we were a mistake.

I looked up at the thin moon, trying to remember if that was good or bad for the waves. It hung in the sky like a shard of forgotten glass, ready to cut the unwary. I ran my fingers through my hair in exasperation. I couldn't remember and I didn't even really know if he was out on the water.

But now I knew I wouldn't be able to stop pacing this stupid porch or tossing in my stupid bed until I knew he wasn't on that death trap of a boat.

I needed to go to the docks and check.

With a deep breath, I took the stairs as fast as I could and started walking down the beach toward the dock. The ocean whispered against the sand and the breeze ruffled my hair and filled my nose with the scent of moving water.

"Where are you going?" A dark voice asked, coming out from behind a palm tree.

I nearly jumped three stories and was half way to throwing a punch before recognizing the voice.

"Dammit, Elijah!" I gasped, putting my hand over my racing heart to keep it in my chest. "You scared me! Don't you sleep?"

Elijah shrugged like sleep didn't matter. "Where are you going?"

I let out a breath, trying to get my adrenaline under control. "The docks. I just need to see if Leo's boat is there."

Elijah's brow darkened as he left the shadows of the tree and came out into the open. "You're worried about him," he observed. "You think he's on that speed boat."

I nodded. "I just can't shake this feeling..." I ran my hand through my hair. It was heavy with humidity. "If his boat's there, then I'll feel a lot better."

"And if it's not?" Elijah's question was one I didn't want to answer. I paused.

"I don't know," I answered honestly, but my stomach twisted and I thought I might be sick.

"Let's get going then," Elijah said, stepping to the side and waiting for me to catch up with him. I was glad he was with me. Even if he drove me nuts, I knew Elijah always had my back. Even in this. If Leo's boat wasn't there, Elijah would know what to do. He was good at stuff like that.

Together we walked along the beach. Eli moved through the dark like a hunting cat- never tripping or stepping on anything that could give away his position. Me, on the other hand, sounded more like an elephant stampeding through the bush.

It wasn't long before the glow of the lamps on the dock greeted us. My footsteps sounded hollow and doomed as we walked along the wooden planks to where Leo stored his boats.

The stall holding *Speed Demon* was empty.

My heart stalled. My chest collapsed and I couldn't find the air to breathe. Elijah's strong grip found my elbow, keeping me from sinking to my knees. I was glad he had come with me.

"Is there another boat?" he asked, his voice gruff and commanding enough to make me answer.

"Yeah, the Silver Lightning..." I turned from the empty stall and went to the next one. Maybe Elijah knew how to hot-wire a boat and we could go out looking for him. Maybe there was a radio and we could contact him. Maybe he was tied up in that boat because someone had stolen *Speed Demon*.

The last one was rather far-fetched, but I still hoped for it.

But Leo wasn't bound and gagged in the boat. Instead,

Murdoch sat in the driver's seat with this feet propped up on the dash.

"Hey, boss," Murdoch said into his headset, his dark eyes landing on me. "There's a girl here to see you."

I swallowed hard, unable to make out the words coming through the headset. The headset must have been some sort of long distance radio for Leo to communicate while out on the racing boat.

Murdoch nodded at whatever command was given to him, plopping his feet on the deck with a thud. He stood, taking the headset off his head and handing it to me. It looked tiny in his giant hands. I swallowed hard and took it, careful not to drop it in the water.

"Leo?" I asked, my voice shaking. I didn't want to argue again. I just wanted to know he was safe, but somehow, being out on a ridiculously dangerous speedboat in the middle of the night just didn't scream safe to me.

"I'm sorry about earlier." Leo's voice came in crisp and clear over the headset.

"It's okay," I said, leaning against the hull of the boat. "Where are you?"

"I needed to think," he replied over the headset, not really answering my question. "Charlotte, there's something I need to tell you."

"You can tell me anything." I closed my eyes to focus on his voice, visualizing him turning the boat around and driving back. Slowly.

"I'm being blackmailed."

"I kind of figured that out," I told him, rolling my eyes. "Can you tell me about what?"

"It's not something I'm proud of," he said slowly. "But I shouldn't keep it from you. It's keeping it from you that got me blackmailed in the first place."

"Okay." I was a little nervous now. Leo was perfect in my eyes. He was everything I could ever want in a man. The idea that he could have done something so terrible that he could be blackmailed about it is a little intimidating. I hoped he wasn't an ax murderer. I could handle just about anything, just not ax-murderer.

"Do you remember why I don't gamble any more?" he asked. His voice was eerily calm on the radio.

"You said you nearly lost everything," I answered slowly, opening my eyes and looking out at the water as if I might see him coming back. "That it scared you."

"That's right." He paused and then let out a long sigh. "I didn't get a loan for the business, Charlotte."

"What? What loan are you talking about?" I frowned, not following his logic. What did a loan have to do with blackmail?

"The loan that got us started, that had such an amazing interest rate-" He took a deep breath, waiting for me to hate him. "There was no loan."

It took me a moment to put his words together. Leo had gotten us a loan to get the business started. That loan was the reason we had been able to have a successful launch and get the business where it was today. We had just talked about it a couple nights ago at the gala. I remembered the loan, so I was confused as to how there wasn't one.

"But, I wrote checks to pay the interest..." I shook my head, not understanding. It had felt like a real loan at the time.

"You paid *me* the interest." He quickly added, "I put every dime back into the company from those checks, but there was no loan."

I swallowed hard, not really wanting the answer to my next question. I could already guess, but I needed to hear it.

"Where did the money come from then, Leo? If it wasn't a loan, how did we get forty-thousand dollars to start the business?"

"I won it in a football game." The boat engine revved again in the background. "Remember the big state game, when we all had nachos together in my dorm room? The other team was the favorite. In fact, it was supposed to be a blow out, but I got an insider tip that their quarterback was out with an injury."

I remembered the game. I remembered not being able to talk at the end of it for screaming at the players not to blow it. The only reason we won was a field goal in overtime that broke the record for the longest field goal kicked by our team. It was considered the game of the decade- one of the closest, most bet on games in the history of the school.

He stopped, and I could hear him inhale sharply on the other end of the line. "The 4:1 odds were too good to pass up, and we needed the money. I bet nearly all of our business capital on it."

It took everything I had not to gasp and take off the headset.

"The only problem was that their quarterback wasn't the only one out," Leo continued, his voice low and full of regret. "Our star running back was out that day, too. For four hours, I was positive that I had just lost the entire ten-thousand dollars I borrowed to make the bet," he said, finishing the story. He stopped talking and waited for me to say something. "I'm so sorry, Charlotte."

Ten thousand dollars. Now, that was hardly any money to us, but back then, it was every dime Bastian, Leo, and Gabe had. They had saved for months working odd jobs and eating nothing but ramen. It had been everything back then.

And Leo had bet it all.

"You never said anything..." I was still processing the implications. Leo had bet all of the money without asking anyone. If the kicker had missed... Our business never would have existed.

"How could I?" Leo's voice cracked. "You looked at me like I was hero when I said we had forty-grand. I didn't want you to look at me like a gambler. I didn't want you to see the real me."

I remembered how happy I had been. How happy everyone had been when Leo said we had a forty-thousand dollar loan to start the company. Leo had been the hero for weeks. I could only imagine the guilt he carried knowing that he was lying to us about where he got the money.

"It's what made me quit gambling. A gust of wind, an untied shoelace, and I could have lost everything." His voice pleaded for understanding and forgiveness. "I had hoped no one would ever know. That it would just disappear and I'd be forever known as the man who got a loan. Not the man who risked his friend's dreams without even asking."

"And the blackmailer found this out?" I asked, trying to keep my head on straight. This definitely did change the way I viewed Leo. For all these years, I'd thought that he'd begged the banks or found a rich uncle to borrow the funds. But just risking everything without even asking? I could see why he didn't want anyone to find out.

"Yes. The longer I let it go, the more successful we were because of the extra money, the more ashamed I was of it." He sighed. "When the blackmail started, they only wanted a little bit of money. When you have a billion dollars, a hundred grand is pocket change."

I nodded. It was strange how keeping a ten thousand dollar bet quiet was worth hundreds of thousands, but money was no object to Leo now. It was no longer about the amount, but what had happened and making sure that people weren't hurt by it. It wasn't just me that would be furious. That money had been Gabe and Bastian's.

I took a deep breath. I didn't know what to think, though I could feel the fury building in my stomach. I closed my eyes, trying to center myself.

"What about the slush fund?" I asked. "You said that it was related to the blackmail? Are you using it to pay the blackmail?"

"I promise you, I had nothing to do with the slush fund's missing money," he said quickly. "But I can't tell you more on the radio. I need to talk to you in person."

"Okay." I opened my eyes and looked around. Murdoch had his arms crossed and was pretending to sleep in the driver's seat while Elijah leaned nonchalantly against a pylon, managing to look relaxed and deadly at the same time. "Well, I'm here by your boat with just these two scary men watching me. I'm not happy about what you just told me, Leo. But, I'll be here."

Leo revved the engine. "I'm coming back in. Will you give the headset back to Murdoch?"

"Leo, be careful," I blurted out. I knew he would be, but I needed to say it.

"I'll go slow," he promised. I could hear the promise in his voice and I knew he meant it. Or at least, he meant slow for him. "Charlotte?"

"Yes?"

"I didn't take that money." He paused, and I heard the boat engine rev again. "I think I know who did though."

"You can tell me when you get here," I told him. "Just get here."

"One more thing," Leo said. "I love you, Charlotte. I have for a long time."

I smiled without thinking, wishing that he didn't melt me so easily. I was angry, but he was on that dangerous boat that I hated. The boat that only added to my nightmares of being left alone. I didn't want my last words to him to be those of anger. "I love you, too, Leo."

With a lump in my throat the size of Texas, I pulled off the headset and handed it back to Murdoch.

"Okay, boss." Murdoch picked up a tablet from the passenger seat and tapped it twice. "Computer says you're lagging slightly on the right. Be sure to compensate."

I put my hands on the side of the boat, trying to keep my thoughts from spinning so wildly in my head. Leo was on his way back and he had an idea of who took the money.

Blackmail. I hated the word.

I took a deep breath. This was a lot to process. The man I loved had done a terrible thing. Granted, he wasn't an ax-murderer, but he had done something worth blackmailing over. I hated the way my stomach clenched when I thought of how he had kept this a secret all these years. Yet, the guilt of that decision had eaten away at him for the past five years to the point where he thought he didn't deserve me.

I hit the side of the boat with the palm of my hand, needing to vent the frustration. How could Leo have done this? He had been perfect until now.

I knew the answer, but I still needed to ask the question. He had done it to make his friends enough money to start their business. It was done with the best intentions. He had saved us, even if he had risked everything to do it.

I hated the shades of gray that left me. What he had done was wrong, but had created the right outcome. He had made all our lives better because of his arrogance. If he had just told us all from the beginning, none of this would have happened.

I had to wonder, would Bastian and Gabe have signed off on the bet if Leo had just asked? I wasn't sure. It was possible. Bastian and Gabe were risk-takers. There was a chance that Leo could have done it with their blessing. I wasn't sure if that lessened his guilt or not.

Not really, I decided. He should have asked. He should have told us instead of calling it a loan. Just because I understood *why* he did it didn't mean I agreed with him.

And now he was being blackmailed. And the slush fund was still an issue.

What if they were connected? Whoever knew this secret of Leo's would have to be close to him, maybe even close enough to access his money. I knew we gave limited access to secretaries and assistants when we had big projects or big clients to woo.

Could one of them still have access?

I shook my head. That didn't make any sense. The accountants were too careful and the passwords changed too often. It had to just be a coincidence. With the app coming out, someone must have just forgotten to mention a big dinner or an emergency flight to the accountants. It honestly wasn't that much money in relation to what billionaires could spend, so it had to just be some sort of oversight.

I sighed and looked over at Murdoch. He was frowning at the tablet and telling Leo something about one of his engines. I hoped Leo got here soon. Maybe, once I could talk to him in person, I would feel better. Maybe I wouldn't feel so lied to.

"Mr. Westbrook?" Murdoch's concerned tone caught my attention. "Leo?"

"What's going on?" I asked, the pit of my stomach

suddenly falling. Cold dread swept over me. Something bad had just happened.

"Leo!" Murdoch shouted into the headset. He shook his head and looked at me. "The radio just went dead. It's probably just a glitch in the system. It should be back up in a minute." He held out his hand to stop me, but the flicker of terror deep in his eyes told me the truth.

"Leo..." I whispered. Cold dread filled me and I shivered in the tropical heat, getting goosebumps up and down my arms. Something bad had happened to him. I prayed it was just my imagination getting the better of me, but deep in my heart, I knew.

He had crashed.

25

———

The sun slowly lifted her radiant head out of the dark ocean, sending light to cast out the shadows of night. I knew it would be warmer soon, but I was still cold with dread. I hugged my arms around me tighter, watching the rays of light bounce off the water and shimmer with hope. Maybe with the dawn they would find him.

I stared out at the water, watching the waves and trying really hard not to think of sharks.

The coast guard will find him, I told myself, repeating like a mantra. If I said it enough times, it had to be true. They would find him, sitting there grinning in his boat, totally fine- just with a dead battery. Not scattered across the ocean with the debris of his shattered boat.

He wouldn't leave me alone. He *wouldn't*. Leo loved me. He wouldn't do the thing I feared most in the world. He wouldn't leave me, especially not after telling me what he had done.

I needed to talk to him. I needed to tell him that I

forgave him. This empty, hollow, sick feeling in the pit of my stomach was terrible and all I knew was that I wanted him safe. I didn't care what he had done anymore. I just wanted him back with me.

I closed my eyes, the sun now too bright to look at. I was so tired. After Leo's radio signal stopped, Murdoch immediately called the coast guard. I'd spent the rest of the night pacing the docks, waiting for a boat to find him. Unfortunately, *Speed Demon* was a very fast boat. There was a lot of territory to search.

I could hear the conversation of the command center over the sound of the water. It was still quiet on the docks with just the sea birds starting to cry that the day was here, so it was hard not to hear the searchers' conversations. Their words floated through my mind. I didn't want to understand the depth of their meaning, because nothing they said gave me hope.

"He was only going fifty knots, and the water was smooth..."

"We found the GPS transponder. It appears to have broken off and gotten caught in the current. It'll take some time to find him..."

"If he crashed going sixty-five miles per hour, that's still a hard crash..."

"He's an experienced captain, perhaps he bailed out in time..."

I thought again of asking Murdoch for the keys to the *Silver Lightning*, but I knew it wouldn't help. I wasn't trained and I'd just get in the way of the coast guard. They had asked me to stay here, to be a point of contact if they did find him. I couldn't just take a boat I didn't know how to drive out into the ocean with no idea what I was doing.

Then they'd just have two people to look for. As much as I hated it, I had to stay on land. Even as useless as I felt, it was where I needed to be.

I turned away from the voices. I just wanted to wake up and find this was all a dream. A horrible, terrible nightmare of a dream. I wanted to just wake up in Leo's bed and find it was yesterday. No blackmail, no missing money, no fight, no crash.

"Here," Murdoch said softly. I opened my eyes to see him holding out a blanket. I stared at it without moving and so he unfolded and carefully wrapped it around my shoulders. "You're shivering. You look exhausted. Go to the *Silver Lightning* and lay down. I'll come get you as soon as there's any word."

"But..." I turned to look back at the command center the coast guard had set up to centralize the search. I didn't want to leave. What if something happened? I needed to be here.

I looked up into Murdoch's eyes, expecting to find hardness and anger. Instead, I found big brown eyes that were warm and gentle. There was a hardness to his face, but a deep well of kindness bubbled deep within his dark eyes. I'd always seen him as cold and intimidating, but in this morning sun, he had a warmth I hadn't expected. Especially from someone who bet all of our friends that Leo and I would never be a couple.

"He would want me to take care of you," Murdoch said quietly, putting his hands on my shoulders and gently steering me away and toward the *Silver Lightning*. "You need to rest."

"Okay," I relented, letting my feet move without thinking. Everything in my brain was foggy and distant from trying not to think and worry, yet still failing. I moved on autopilot because if I thought about what was happening, I would break down.

I couldn't break down yet. Not until I knew for sure.

"Do you know why I bet that the two of you would never get together?" Murdoch asked after a moment. The sounds of the command center were fading to the gentle bumps and splashes of boats tied to a dock.

I shook my head. "No." Something deep in my chest started to ache.

"It's because I have to win," Murdoch stated. "I'm an ex gambler- that's how Leo found me. I used to work security at some rather disreputable gambling establishments. I was in a bad place until Leo got me a real job and out of gambling. He saved me."

"I didn't know that," I said, fighting against the lump in my throat. I wondered just how many others Leo had saved that I didn't know about. Knowing that Leo had helped him out of a terrible position suddenly made Murdoch's unwavering loyalty make more sense, but not why he wouldn't want me in Leo's life.

"He's a good man." Murdoch looked at me, his eyes telling me that he believed it far more than words could. "That's why you were my last bet. I bet that you and Leo would never be a couple."

My stomach clenched. He didn't think I was good for Leo.

"Why don't you want us together?" I asked, tightening the blanket around my shoulders and looking anxiously for Elijah. Suddenly, being alone with Murdoch didn't seem like such a good idea.

"I *do* want you together. You make him happy, and he deserves some happiness," Murdoch replied. "But, you see, I have to win."

We'd reached the boat. I clutched at the blanket and turned to face him, doing my best to be brave. I didn't think he would hurt me, but he was loyal to Leo, not me.

"I don't understand," I said. "How can you want him to be happy with me, but bet that we'd never be together?"

"I made the bet, because if you didn't end up together, I'd win some money. I would win *something*. But money would just be a consolation prize," he explained. He smiled, the planes of his face warming into something that was no longer frightening. "But, the two of you together and in love? That's real winning. It's better than money."

"So, you bet that we would never fall in love, even though you really did want us to?" I frowned trying to figure it out. It was a little backward, but I could follow the logic. If he won the bet, he would be sad but rich. If he lost the bet, he'd be happy but poor. Either way, he won in some fashion.

"Yes," Murdoch replied. He put his hand gently on my shoulder. "You should know, that as far as I'm concerned, I won. I got the outcome that I wanted."

The world didn't seem quiet so cold and frightening for a moment. If people like Murdoch were rooting for us, how could anything bad happen? Leo had to be safe. "Thank you, Murdoch."

He nodded and offered me his hand to get into the boat. I climbed aboard and settled into the passenger seat, wrapping the blanket around me. For a moment, I considered starting up the boat and searching anyway, but I was so tired I could barely see straight. At this point, I'd be more likely to run him over than find him. Murdoch waited until I was settled before nodding.

"I'll let Elijah know you're here, and I'll come get you as soon as there's any updates," he promised. He smiled at me fondly. "I know it's hard, but try and get some rest. We'll find him."

I yawned, my jaws cracking with the size of it. The sun was so warm now, and this seat was surprisingly comfortable... maybe if I just closed my eyes for a moment, it would all just go away...

26

Charlotte...

Leo's voice hovered on the morning light, caressing me with warmth and feelings of home.

"Leo?" I whispered, blinking my eyes against the light and waking from sleep. Was he here? Was he safe?

I rubbed my eyes to find myself alone. No one was there, not even Murdoch or Eli. Just me, alone and dreaming in a boat.

I stifled a sigh and forced the tears back. I hadn't cried yet and I wasn't about to now. Crying didn't solve anything. Crying was for when things were finished and safe. Crying was for when there was nothing else to do. I wasn't finished yet. Leo wasn't finished yet. So I wasn't crying yet.

I looked down at my watch to see a little more than an hour had passed. There had to be some sort of update by now, but I expected that Murdoch was trying to let me sleep. It was a sweet gesture, but I needed to know where the man I loved was, even if they weren't sure.

I stood up and stretched my arms overhead, hearing a disturbing number of pops and crunches in my shoulders.

The chair was not designed for sleeping in, but I at least felt a little more refreshed than I had an hour ago.

My phone buzzed in my pocket. I had completely forgotten about it. I turned on the screen to see several worried messages from Bastian and Gabe, some work emails that could wait until later, and a game notification. I put it back in my pocket with a sigh. I hadn't been expecting a text message from Leo with his exact geographical coordinates, but I had hoped he had tried to contact me that way.

I jumped out of the boat and walked along the dock. Now that it was daylight, there was far more activity. Men in uniform buzzed around looking important the closer I got to the command center, but nothing seemed to have changed. The sky was the same hopeful shade of blue that it always was and the dark waves rolled in just the same. The same level of determination and activity, with no big smiles or bright eyes told me that there was nothing new.

I stopped and just stood there. *What would I do without Leo? What would any of us do?* My heart was slowly breaking, being squeezed in a vice with every second I didn't know where he was. I didn't know how long my heart would survive before it shattered.

I turned from the command center, thinking I would go find Murdoch, when I saw a boat was coming in. It was one of the coast guard vessels, but something about it drew my attention. I stared out at it, shadowing my eyes from the sun and wishing it was just a little bit closer.

Someone was standing at the bow of the ship. Someone with unruly brown hair and broad shoulders.

My heart knew before my eyes. It was Leo.

I ran to the edge of the dock, thinking of jumping off and swimming to the ship just to have those extra few moments with him, but I stayed put and just wished for wings.

Leo was alive.

All my anger disappeared in a breath. I didn't have time to be angry any more. Just time for loving him and having that man in my life. I wasn't going to let one stupid mistake five years ago ruin everything. Not when he was everything to me.

The big boat lumbered in far too slowly for my taste, and apparently for Leo's as well. Long before the boat was tied down or even fully finished stopping, he was jumping from the side of the boat and onto the dock.

I ran to him, throwing my arms around him and holding onto him for dear life. He pulled me into him, kissing my hair. I breathed in the scent of him, mixed with ocean and sweat, but taking every inch of him in with my senses to know he was really here and this wasn't a dream.

"Charlotte," he whispered, pressing his lips against mine and making sure I was real, too. He was firm and real, and clinging to me as strongly as I clung to him.

That's when I started to cry.

"I thought I lost you," I sobbed, tears running down my cheeks. Tears of relief mingled with tears of stress and concern. He was alive. He hadn't left me. We still had our whole future in front of us. "What happened? Are you okay?"

"I'll live. I thought I lost *you*," he replied. His eyes went to my tears and he frowned, wincing at the motion. There was a large cut over his eye that was no longer bleeding, but looked painful. He put his hand to my cheek and wiped them away with the rough pad of his thumb. "I've never seen you cry before."

I sniffled, and wiped the tears with the back of my hand, embarrassed. I wished I could be a little stronger. People were starting to stare at the rescued man and his bawling girlfriend. Leo was fine. He was the one who had just survived a boat crash, and if the myriad of cuts and bruises were any indication, he had far more reason to be upset than I did. He was alive and safe. There was no need for tears, yet I couldn't stop them.

Leo leaned forward and kissed me again. I could taste my tears in his kiss, salty and full of emotion. He pulled back after a moment, his blue eyes going to mine. "You are so beautiful."

"Even when I'm crying?" I laughed, knowing that I was anything but beautiful right now. I'd been up for over twenty-four hours straight with just a quick nap. I hadn't eaten since dinner and I sorely needed a cup of coffee. There was no way I was beautiful with that on my plate and then adding tears, red eyes, splotchy cheeks, and a runny nose.

He touched my cheek, his fingers gentle and kind. There were tears in his eyes. "Always. You are always beautiful to me."

When he looked at me like that, with the sun in his hair and his eyes so blue the sky paled behind him, I had to believe him. Even with my tangled hair and wrinkled t-shirt, I knew he was telling the truth. I was beautiful to him.

"Excuse me, ma'am," a male voice said with a light touch on my shoulder. I turned to see a paramedic behind me. He looked at Leo. "Sir, we need to get you to the hospital."

"Of course!" I said, leaping to the side and practically pushing Leo in the paramedic's direction. I had been so wrapped up in just seeing him that I had forgotten that he had just crashed his boat.

I followed Leo and the paramedic to the waiting ambulance, noting how he limped slightly on his left foot, how he cradled his left arm, the bruises already forming on the back of his legs and the myriad of cuts and scratches I was just now noticing.

He was banged up to hell and back. A lump rose in the back of my throat again, the panic of losing him welling up within me. Fresh tears rolled down my cheeks as I thought of how close he must have come to dying.

The paramedic got him into the truck and strapped him into the ambulance.

"I want her to come with me," Leo said, as I stood outside the ambulance door. "If she'll come."

The request melted my sore heart.

The paramedic nodded. "Hop on in."

"You couldn't get me off this ambulance if you tried," I told the paramedic.

"I was afraid you wouldn't want anything to do with me," Leo said quietly as I crawled inside and sat down next to him.

"What happened, Leo?" I asked, changing the topic. I wasn't ready to talk about that yet. I just wanted to be happy that he was alive for a little longer before having to be angry again.

"Well, I certainly didn't mean to crash," Leo teased with a a wink. He sighed when he saw me frowning. "I'm not one hundred percent sure how it happened. The engine was acting up, and then something just slipped."

"I'm just glad you're okay," I said firmly, clicking my seat belt into place. There was so much that I wanted to talk to him about, but, I knew that most of it wasn't something we should discuss in front of the paramedic.

"Me too," Leo agreed. He took my hand in his and squeezed. I knew he was thinking the same things I was. "I'll tell you more, later."

The paramedic checked to make sure we were all set.

"The Coast Guard said they checked your immediate injuries, but that you probably had some broken bones. We'll get you to the hospital and have you checked out. I have to say that you look to be in great shape for being out on the open ocean all night."

"Luckily, that boat has some pretty insane safety measures," Leo replied as the paramedic sat down with us. His partner started the engine and the ambulance stated to rumble forward.

"Yeah, except for a crappy radio and an easily broken-off GPS," I grumbled. "You know, I really, *really*, really hate that boat now."

Leo chuckled. "I promise not to get another one."

"Good," I said. "I don't know why you liked it so much in the first place."

"I do." Leo paused, swallowing hard. He took a deep breath, and looked at me with shame and defeat in his eyes. "The boat, the speed- it was gambling."

"What?" I wasn't quite sure how driving a boat was the same as putting money on a horse. This felt like another confession and I wasn't sure I wanted to hear it.

"It was gambling. Not with money, but with my life. It gave me the same rush." Leo looked down, shame pinking his cheeks for a moment before looking back up at me. "I'm sorry."

I was just so glad that he was safe, I would have forgiven just about anything at this point. This was an easy thing to forgive. I reached out and took his hand, giving it a squeeze. "I love you, Leo. No matter what."

He brought my hand to his lips and kissed it. Relief oozed out of his smile as he held my hand close to him. I knew it wasn't a proud moment for him, and I knew that just admitting what he had done was difficult. He had replaced one addiction for another, but at least he was realizing it.

"I love you, Charlotte," he whispered. "You were all I thought of while I was out there."

Tears threatened to overwhelm me again. "No scaring me like that again."

"Never again," he promised, his grip tightening on my hand. "I'm never leaving you again."

27

It was hot outside the main entrance of the hospital as I helped Leo into the car to leave. The discharge paperwork was finally signed and we were ready to head home to recover from the day.

"Well, that was fun," he remarked, handing his paperwork to Murdoch and going to the open backseat car door. I helped him get settled, chuckling at how he thought the blur of tests, stitches, casts, and medical words was "fun."

"I'm just glad you get to go home tonight," I said as Murdoch closed the car door behind me. I took Leo's hand in mine. He looked absolutely exhausted. Luckily, other than some dehydration, a broken arm, plenty of stitches and more bruises than I could count, the doctors said he was fine. They still wanted him watched overnight as they hadn't ruled out a concussion, but they were confident he would make a full recovery.

"Me too. There are some perks to having access to a personal physician who can provide all the hospital requirements in the comfort of your own home," he replied, leaning back in his seat and closing his eyes. There was a large bandage on his forehead and the blue of his sling was garish against the black leather car interior. "Remind me to thank Bastian for recommending Dr. Verner. I hate hospitals."

"We're all set," I called up to Murdoch in the driver's seat. I could see a light smile in his eyes reflected in the rear view mirror as he pulled away from the hospital. Murdoch was definitely growing on me.

"You know where to go, Murdoch," Leo added.

"We'll be there in just a few minutes," Murdoch informed us. The road wasn't busy, which was wonderful and the silence after the incessant beeping of the hospital was most welcome.

Finally, for the first time in hours, we weren't surrounded by people. I could finally find out the questions burning inside of me about the blackmail.

"Leo, what is the connection with the slush fund and the blackmail?" I asked after a moment. I knew I should let him rest, but I had been waiting to find out for hours now.

He sighed, slowly opening his blue eyes and sitting up. "That wasn't me, Charlotte. I didn't take that money out," Leo replied. I could see the honesty in his eyes as he reached for my hands and then paused, not wanting to push me. He swallowed hard. "But they are related. You said it was my authorization code on the account?"

I nodded.

"There's only one person who would access to that code, other than me." Leo's face hardened. "And he wouldn't know that it's tracked so closely. And he needs the money."

"Who?" I asked. I didn't have any ideas.

"Toby." Leo's voice was flat and cold.

"Your assistant?" I asked. It wouldn't be that strange for Leo to give Toby his access code for a business trip, especially during busy times, like now with the app launch. I knew I had used the slush fund twice in the past month for emergency flights for myself and Bastian. "But why would he need the money?"

"I gave him my code last week when we were working," he explained. Leo ran his good hand through his hair, making it stand on end. "He's got a bad history with gambling. I think he's in debt and needed a way to pay it off."

I thought of how I had seen Leo and Toby come out of the Gamblers Anonymous meeting. If he was gambling, he would need access to money. I knew Leo paid him well, but I could only imagine how easy it would be to lose it all.

"Is he a gambler?" I asked, wanting to make sure I was right about him.

"Yes. I met Toby my sophomore year of college at a poker game," Leo answered. "He was the one who showed me how to bet on sports games. He was awful at it. Honestly, you could just pick the opposite of whatever he did and usually win."

"What makes you think he's gambling again?"

"Little things. I know his habits." Leo tried to smooth down his hair with his hand, but gave up. "I gave him this job when he came to me a few years ago. He was in debt to some rather scary individuals when he came to me for help. He was desperate, and I could see myself in his situation. If I had lost our start-up money, I could have been him. We were the same coin, just different faces."

"So that's how he became your assistant. I'd always wondered," I said. Leo frowned. "I mean, he's got strong skills, but there were always better applicants. I can see why you picked him."

"Thing were good." Leo shrugged. "And then he came to me a few months ago. He'd gotten back into bad habits."

"And you helped him again." I smoothed out the fabric of my shorts with my palms. They were all wrinkled from wearing them all night.

"Yes. I helped him pay off his new debt and get back in the program." Leo shook his head and sighed. "But I made it very clear that I wasn't happy. The whole point of helping him get this job was to give him a way out. I told him never again. Bailouts are not the answer, even with unlimited money."

"And now, he's back in debt, but he can't come to you," I said, putting the pieces together. "Which is why he took the money from the slush fund. He didn't know it was so closely monitored, and he was hoping to just replace it before it was noticed."

"That's what I think as well," Leo agreed.

"But what about the blackmail? How would he know about the bet you made in college?" I asked. "How did he know it was something you would be willing to pay to keep quiet?"

"He would know because he was there when I made the bet. I didn't think he saw how much I won, but apparently he did." Leo's jaw twitched as he tightened it. "He put the pieces together and realized that my 'loan' was that bet. It doesn't take a genius to figure the rest out. Especially how I feel about you."

"And now you think he's blackmailing you." I hated the way it sounded. I hated the way it made my stomach knot up. I wished I could just fix all of it and make it so that Leo was perfect again.

But I couldn't. I knew the truth now.

"But how do you know it's him? He could just be a thief, not a blackmailer," I pressed.

"I had Murdoch check his phone records and follow up." Leo's eyes caught a predatory gleam. "He didn't cover his tracks very well once Murdoch pushed a few people. It's him."

I fell back into the seat, numb. How could Toby do this? Leo had done everything he could to help Toby and yet Toby was throwing it back in his face. Blackmail. Theft.

"If you had just told us about the bet five years ago, none of this would have happened," I blurted out. I was so tired I wasn't censoring my words any more. It wasn't the kindest thing to say, but it was true. "All you had to do was tell us where the loan money really came from, Leo."

"I'm so sorry, Charlotte." He took a shaky breath. Defeat hung on his shoulders. "You're absolutely right, though. You have no idea how many times I tried to tell you. How many times I tried to tell Bastian. I told Gabe once when he was drunk, but he didn't believe me."

"You should have told me," I replied, my voice heated but the anger was burned out. I had been so worried about him that I wasn't angry anymore.

"You wouldn't have looked at me the same." Leo turned. "Do you see why I pushed you away for so long? You deserve someone better than me."

"I don't want anyone else," I said stubbornly. I stared at the floor for a moment, but needing to put voice to the hurt in my heart. I trusted Leo. Up until today, I didn't know of a single lie he ever told me. But this lie was huge. "But you did lie to me. To my brother and your friend."

"I hated lying," Leo confessed, his face falling. "To everyone, but especially you. You'd look at me with so much trust everyday and I knew I was nothing but a liar. It's why I never let myself have you. You deserve someone that doesn't lie. I'd understand if you never wanted to see me again."

I looked over at him, ready to tell him he was right. But, when I looked at him, I didn't see a man who lied to me.

I saw a man who loved me. Who had tried every day since that day to make it up to all of his friends. A man who helped others. A man with demons but who was determined to fight them. I saw the way he always went above and beyond without being obvious about it. The small things he did to make the world a better place, ever asking for recognition or payment.

He was a good man who made a mistake.

But mostly, I saw love. I saw that he was a human being who loved me. I didn't want to be mad anymore. I had already forgiven him. He wasn't completely off the hook, but if I had made the same mistake, I would hope he would see past it and forgive me. So, I was going to forgive him. He had his heart in the right place, even if he hadn't gone about it in the right way.

He was no longer perfect in my eyes. He was human, and in a way that made him so much better. He was real. *We* were real. I wasn't perfect, and now neither was he. He had lost his god-like status in my mind, which meant we could have a future together because we were both mere mortals.

"Leo." I picked up his good hand and held it in mine. I loved the way it felt. The weight of his palm against mine and the rough pads of his fingertips. "It was a mistake a long time ago. Yeah, I'm a little angry, but... I love you. I don't want anyone else. I never have."

"I don't want there to be any secrets between us," Leo replied. His eyes were bright with emotion. "I love you. I don't want to keep anything from you ever again."

"You need to tell Bastian and Gabe. They deserve to know, too."

"I know. I plan on it." Fear flickered across his face followed by resolve. "Will you help me?"

"Always," I promised. I meant it, too.

"Thank you, Charlotte." He smiled and squeezed my hand. "I love you. So much."

"I love you." I squeezed his hand. I wiped at my eyes, wanting to change the subject. I had enough of deep emotions for the day. I needed to laugh, not cry anymore. "I should tell you something, though. Since we're not keeping secrets anymore."

"What?" Concern crossed his face at my serious tone. "You can tell me anything."

"I totally ate your sandwich that day in the office last week. It wasn't the secretary. It was me," I confessed.

Leo laughed, breaking the tension building in the car.

"I don't know, Charlotte," he said, smiling at my joke. "I was very fond of that sandwich."

"I'll get you another. An even better sandwich," I promised, loving that he was joking with me again. Things were slowly righting themselves in my world.

"You already have," he replied. "You've given me so much."

The car pulled up in front of the beach mansion Bastian and I were staying at. I frowned, thinking we were supposed to be going to Leo's place. That's where the doctor was meeting us.

"Murdoch? What are we doing here?" I asked.

"Charlotte, I need to ask you a favor," Leo answered for him. "I need you to call an emergency board meeting."

"A meeting?" I repeated. I was expecting that he needed me to go get Bastian or that he wanted to stay with me for the night. I wasn't expecting him to ask me for a board meeting. Especially because he could call a board meeting on his own. He didn't need me to do it for him.

"Yes. An emergency board meeting." He smiled hopefully. "In Miami. As soon as possible."

"Okay..." I frowned, not yet understanding what he was doing. "Why don't you just call it? And, you don't have to call a board meeting to tell Bastian and Gabe about this. Just come inside and tell them right now. It'll suck, but they'll understand."

He shook his head. "I need you to do it. I need you to be worried about my personal history interfering with my work."

"I do? But why would I do that? I don't believe it does..." Slowly, what Leo was doing dawned on me. "Oh, I get it. I'll call the meeting and Toby's going to panic. He might even do something stupid. Like confess to the blackmail."

"And hopefully the slush fund theft." He squeezed my hand, giving me confidence in his plan to catch Toby red-handed. "Plus, since we'll be in Miami..."

"We'll be in US jurisdiction," I finished. I pulled out my phone and dialed the familiar number of Bastian's secretary. "Hi Gladys, I need to call an emergency meeting of the board..."

28

I hadn't been able to eat anything all morning. My stomach was made of knots and snakes, and the snakes weren't happy about the knots.

I stood in front of the main table in the empty meeting room and tugged on the non-existent wrinkles of my suit jacket. I'd been tugging on it all morning to the point where I was afraid the shoulder seams might give out. It was just nerves. I'd been in hundreds of important meetings, but this one was different. This wasn't just money on the line. This was Leo. I was nervous. Crazy nervous.

I just had to stick to the plan.

I took a deep breath and went over to the coffee station on the side of the room. A big pot of fresh coffee was already sitting and waiting. I took one of the mugs and poured the dark liquid along with my requisite two creams and sugars. Maybe some caffeine would help me settle.

"Hi, Charlotte," Toby greeted me. I nearly jumped out of my skin. I hadn't heard him come in. Luckily, my coffee was sitting on the counter so I could stir it, or it would have ended up all over me. That wouldn't have helped my nerves.

"Hi, Toby," I stuttered. I did my best to smile, but what I really wanted to do was rip his head off. Here he was, smiling and acting all friendly, when in reality he was blackmailing his employer. "How are you?"

Toby reached for a mug. He was already sweating and I doubted hot coffee would help him. "I'm doing fine. I'd rather be out on a beach than here, but..." He shrugged. "That's the job, right? Got to do what the boss man says."

"Yeah," I half-heartedly agreed. I swallowed on a dry throat. "Hey, Toby? Do you know if Leo's used the CEO slush fund for anything recently?"

Toby wiped his forehead with his sleeve before dropping a creamer in his coffee. He refused to raise his eyes to mine, instead staring into his drink. "I'm not sure. Why?"

I did my best to keep my face calm. I suddenly had a new respect for actors. This was hard. "The accountants are on me for it. There's money missing from the account."

"Well, it's a slush fund, right? Money's always moving around in those." Toby sipped on his coffee. "Besides, they're billionaires. I doubt it's anything. It's not like they're going to miss a few dollars out of their Scrooge McDuck swimming pool vaults."

"I'd agree with you, except not for this account." I shrugged, trying to make it not sound like I was accusing him. "Due to how easy it would be to hide money in this account, the accountants are anal about it. They have to have receipts for everything. They track every dollar. This isn't the cash box for the secretaries where ten bucks won't be missed. This is a special funds account. They watch it down to the penny."

"They do?" Toby paled and his hand shook slightly, spilling his coffee down the side of his cup. His Adam's apple bobbed as he dry-swallowed. If I hadn't been sure it was him, this reaction at least told me he was panicked. No wonder he was a terrible gambler. The man had no poker face and a billion tells.

"Yeah. It was Leo's account authorization that took the money out, so I was hoping you might know what it was. The accountants are tracking where he logged in from and where the money went. They're really on my butt about it." I lowered my voice and glanced around the room. "It's part of why I called the meeting today. Your boss is in some serious trouble."

I so deserved an Oscar for this. Even though I was shaking in my shoes, I was somehow managing to control my blushing and keep my voice even.

Toby's eyes widened. "What do you mean? What's else is he in trouble for?"

"I shouldn't... it'll all come out in the meeting." I bit my lower lip, wondering if I was overplaying it. Toby seemed to be eating up my worry with a spoon, though. Maybe I did have a future in film. I rubbed my forehead like I was getting a tension headache. "This is going to be a crappy meeting."

"I didn't realize that so much was wrong. Are you okay?" Toby asked, his mousy face furrowing into a concerned frown.

"Not really," I answered with a big sigh. "I found out that Leo's been keeping a big secret about how Kindling Dating was founded. I don't know exactly what it is, I just overheard him on the phone the other day. When I asked him about it, we had a big fight. I'm hoping he'll just come clean during the meeting today."

"So you don't know what he did?" Toby looked far too hopeful.

I shrugged and hugged my arms around me. "I know it has something to do with some money. Then, this whole slush fund money going missing? I know they're related. I'm just hoping that he'll come clean and let us help him. Even though we had a big fight, I still love him, you know?"

Toby patted my shoulder, but it was obvious his thoughts were elsewhere. "I'm sure he'll do the right thing. I know you mean a lot to him."

"Enough that he won't tell me anything?" I scoffed. "From what I've figured out, it's bad. It might not be a bad idea to take a look at your resume. I don't think this is going to go well."

"Thanks..." Toby's voice shook at the prospect of not only losing his job but his blackmail gravy train.

I patted his shoulder and he shrunk away slightly. I couldn't believe he bought my performance. I felt like I was the worst liar in the world. There were so many holes in the story I just told, but the shaky way he was playing with his coffee cup made me believe he thought it was the truth.

I turned and headed for the table, trying hard not to giggle with nervousness. Hopefully, he would slip up. The thought of losing his job hopefully would make him nervous and he would get a little desperate. We needed him to speak without thinking.

The door opened and Bastian and Gabe walked in, confident and well dressed. They looked like businessmen instead of beach bums today.

"You realize I should be on a beach with a beautiful woman right now?" Bastian informed me as he flopped into one of the leather chairs and gave me a displeased look.

"Sorry to make you actually work," I retorted.

"Luckily for me, there are beaches and beautiful women here in Miami," Gabe chimed in, taking a seat across from Bastian. He grinned at me. "So, at least I'm not mad at you, Charlotte."

"I appreciate that, Gabe," I replied, taking a sip of my coffee.

Gabe's assistant, an older woman who was always showing off pictures of her grandkids, came in and sat in the chair next to him. I smiled at her, knowing that she considered Gabe one of her own children. There was no way she'd ever do this kind of thing to Gabe. But then again, I never thought Toby would do this either.

We were just waiting on Leo now. Anxiety gnawed in my stomach and sat heavy on my chest.

"Hey, assistant," Bastian barked at me. "Will you get me some coffee?"

I crossed my arms and glared at him. "What's the magic word, *boss*?"

"Paycheck." Bastian grinned at me to show me that he was just playing. He could read the tension written all over my face and was just trying to make me focus on him instead of being nervous. He was always looking out for me.

I rolled my eyes at him, but poured him a cup and put it in front of him. "You can get your own cream and sugar for what you pay me."

Gabe snickered and his assistant's eyes widened slightly, but she didn't say anything.

That's when the door opened and Leo limped in.

The bruises on his face were starting to set in and he looked like hell. Seeing him all beat up made my heart hurt. I wished there was a way that I could take some of his pain away. He just looked so broken that it made what I was going to have to do next that much harder.

Leo didn't say anything. He just took his place at the table, clutching his broken arm tight to his body, the pain obvious on his face. He looked broken. It took everything I had not to look at him. We had to pretend like we were fighting for this to be believable to Toby.

I cleared my throat and stood at the head of the table. "Now that we're all here, I'd like to thank you all for coming."

"We didn't really have much of a choice," Gabe murmured under his breath and I gave him a dirty look. He plastered innocence on his face.

"Anyway, I called this meeting because some information has come to light." My voice caught. I knew that this was what needed to be said, but the words didn't want to come out. I hated this so much. Even though it was a show to get Toby to confess, I struggled with the words. "I... Leo, he..."

"Charlotte... please..." The way Leo said my name broke my heart. I knew this was all a show to get Toby to confess, but it sounded real. I nearly broke.

"I have to, Leo," I whispered. "I'm mad at you."

"I have something to say," Leo announced. He stood up and I closed my eyes. I knew what words were coming. "I quit."

Bastian and Gabe both sat up straight in their seats, their leisurely, carefree attitude completely gone. Toby looked ready to throw up. Without Leo, he didn't have a job.

"You can't quit!" Bastian crossed his arms, the scar above his eye going white.

"Well, I can quit or you can fire me," Leo replied, his voice somehow even and calm. "I'd rather quit."

Bastian's eyes narrowed. "What the hell is wrong with you, Leo?" His voice was dangerously low.

Leo took a breath and opened his mouth.

"Leo, think about what you're doing," Toby interjected,

standing up and going over to him. Toby put a hand on his shoulder. "Don't do this."

"I have to, Toby." Leo pushed Toby's hand from his shoulder. "This should have been said a long time ago. It's time to finally come clean."

Toby stared at him, the whites of his eyes going big. If Leo revealed the secret, his blackmail would be worthless.

"Leo, can I talk to you for a second?" Toby asked, pulling Leo to face him. "Before you do this, let me just talk to you. I don't think you've thought this through."

"You know what? He's right, Leo," Gabe said, standing up. "Bastian and I are going to go grab a doughnut. You let your assistant talk some sense into you."

I looked over at Gabe as he and Bastian got up. This wasn't the way things were supposed to go, but it could still work. Gabe's assistant was looking at us like we were all nuts, but she was already halfway out the door.

"You should go with them, Charlotte," Toby said, motioning to the door.

"No, you should stay." Leo was firm. "She already suspects something, Toby. Why do you think she called this meeting?"

Toby glanced back and forth between the two of us, deciding if it was worth pushing Leo. "You can do whatever you want, Charlotte. I'd go if I were you."

"I want to see this through." I crossed my arms. "He should come clean. At least to me."

Toby frowned at me, turning back to face Leo.

"You shouldn't do this, Leo. Charlotte doesn't know anything. She's just being a woman and trying to get back at you for your fight."

I made a scoffing noise and had to cross my arms to keep

from hitting the chauvinistic bastard. *Just being a woman?* I didn't know it was possible to despise someone this much.

"Don't insult her," Leo growled. I wished I could smile. Even with everything on the line, Leo was going to defend me.

Toby changed his tactic. "Imagine what Bastian and Gabe are going to think. They're your friends, but they'll hate you after this." Toby took a deep breath. "I mean, look how Charlotte's reacting. No offense, but she's got you up in front of the board. She's been lovesick about you for years and she's throwing you to the wolves. What are Bastian and Gabe going to do?"

I shook my head in disbelief. Toby still assumed that Leo didn't know the blackmailer was him. If he kept Leo from quitting, he could still keep his cushy job. If he could convince Leo to keep his mouth shut, he could keep his money-making blackmail machine going as well. He was going to gamble on Leo's guilt and try to keep it all.

"Toby, Leo made a huge mistake. He betrayed all of our trust." I crossed my arms and glared at Leo, doing my best to look angry. "I don't think I can ever forgive that. He needs to come clean."

"Charlotte, it was a long time ago," Toby said sharply. "I really think you should leave and let me talk some sense into Leo."

"Talk some sense into him?" I took an angry step forward. "Do you know what he did?"

"Do you?" Toby replied.

"I know enough. I know that he's a liar." I paused. I needed him to contradict me. "I know that *you* helped him."

"What?" Toby shook his head in surprise. "I didn't help him! He made that bet on his own."

"But you told him to," I pushed. "You told him to bet on that game."

"I lost my shirt in that game. He won forty grand and made a billion dollar company. Me? I had to go ask my mom to help me with rent." Toby was mad now. "There's no reason for Leo to have all this and for me to have nothing."

"So you should have won? I don't think you even had the money to make a real bet," I sneered.

Toby's eyes flashed. "Like he did? He took his friends' money. He's no different than me. If he had lost instead of me, you'd wouldn't look at him the way you do."

"So you knew? You knew about the money and the bet?" I let out incredulous sigh. "And you didn't tell anyone either?"

"Oh, I knew." Toby got right up into my face. "I figured it out long before you ever did. If you could just see how guilty he is. He pretends that he's helping people- giving them jobs and going to meetings- but it's just guilt. He's no better than me even if he acts like he is. Someday, everyone will know."

"After you get yours?" I pressed. "You're pathetic."

"Says the woman who hangs her boyfriend out to dry because of a fight," Toby countered. "One fight and you have to go tattle to your brother?"

"My brother isn't a part of this. Why do you deserve to have what Leo does?" I asked, glaring at him. "He worked hard for it."

"Because I deserve it more than he does!" Toby's round face was livid. "He thinks he's all high and mighty because he doesn't gamble anymore. But he's no better than me. He's a fraud. Once I get what I'm owed, everyone will know what he did to get here."

"You just want money? You'd hold this secret over his

head for money?" I hoped I wasn't too obvious, but I need him to say more. "You don't deserve anything!"

"I deserve everything! He fucking owes me!" Toby's voice rose to a yell. "I'll get what I'm owed or I really will tell everyone. I follow through on my threats."

"You deserve everything you get, Toby," I hissed. "You're scum."

Toby laughed. "Like you could ever do anything about it."

"She just did," Leo said quietly. "It's over, Toby."

Toby looked over at him in surprise as if he had forgotten that Leo was there. "What?"

Leo walked to the table and picked up my tablet. He touched a button and suddenly Toby's voice boomed into the room on the speakers. It sounded too high and feminine.

> "Once I get what I'm owed, everyone will know what he did to get here."
>
> "You'd hold this secret over his head for money? You don't deserve anything!"
>
> "I deserve everything! He fucking owes me! I'll get what I'm owed or I really will tell everyone. I follow through on my threats."

Leo tapped the tablet and the room fell silent. Toby's eyes were about to bug out of his head.

"Really, Toby," I said, shaking my head. "You should know we record everything in these rooms. That's how we take minutes. That's the point of having meetings in these rooms."

"You set me up!" Toby blanched and then his round cheeks turned red. "You bitch!"

He lunged for me, but Leo stepped in front of him.

"Touch her and you're a dead man." Leo's voice was low and dangerous. Fire flashed in his blue eyes and his shoulders somehow got bigger and more intimidating. Even with a broken arm and a beat-up face, Leo was determined to be my protector.

Toby stepped back, putting his hands up in the air. If looks could kill, I'd be ten feet under. He looked like he was going to lunge again as soon as Leo moved.

The door to the meeting room opened and Bastian and Gabe sauntered in, followed by three police officers.

"Toby, I think it best you leave with these nice gentlemen," Gabe announced, indicating to the armed guards. "Oh, and yes- we were all outside listening to everything."

"But, how?" Toby searched the room with his eyes, desperately looking for a way out of the situation. As soon as he realized there wasn't one, the fight drained from his body. "He already told you all everything. This was a trap."

"Yes, it was Toby." I crossed my arms. "I'm sorry, but it had to be done."

"I just wanted to win. Just once," Toby whispered as he walked to the door. "It's not fair."

One of the police officers put his hand on Toby's back, leading him out of the room. I watched as the door swung shut and then let out a long sigh of relief and collapsed into a chair. It was done.

"Well, that went well," Bastian observed. "You did a nice job, Charlotte."

"She did a great job," Leo corrected. He moved to stand behind me, putting his good hand on my shoulder. "I need to thank all of you. For helping me with this."

Gabe grinned. "It was actually kind of fun. Though, next

time I want Charlotte's job. I want to be the one who gets the confession."

"There better not be a next time," I told him. "No more secrets."

"Agreed," Bastian, Leo and Gabe said at the same time.

I looked at the three men in my life and smiled. Leo had explained everything to Bastian and Gabe on the plane ride back to Miami. They had actually taken it better than I had, though I was fairly certain the only reason Leo wasn't sporting black eyes from the two of them was because he was already beat up from his accident.

"What happened with that slush fund money?" Gabe asked, picking up one of the mugs and playing with it.

"The accountants tracked it. It was withdrawn for cash from the bank across the street from where Toby was staying. Leo was on the island at the time," I explained. "They did a little more digging, and from what I could understand of their banking-legalese terms, it's pretty obvious that Toby took it for his gambling."

"I wish I could have helped him," Leo said quietly.

"What? They guy just tried to blackmail you and stole money from you, and you wish you could have done more?" Gabe shook his head. "You're too nice, Leo. I'd be doing a tap dance of glee right now."

"I think it's sweet," I countered. "You don't want anybody stuck in that hell."

"You tried, Leo," Bastian said with a shrug. "You can't save everybody."

The fact that Leo still wanted to help Toby, despite everything, showed how good Leo was. He was a good man. I loved him even more. Toby threw away a friendship worth more than anything that blackmail could have given him.

"Well, I need a drink," Gabe announced, putting his

arms across Bastian and Leo's shoulders. "Drinks down at the bar on 13th street?"

"God, yes," I answered. "It's not even ten in the morning, but I want something."

Bastian laughed. "You had a rough week. I should give you the day off or something."

"Yeah, that would be nice," I replied. "You're not going to do it though, are you?"

Bastian thought for a moment, pushing Gabe's arm off his shoulder. "Nah. No day off."

"Just come play hookey with me," Leo whispered. "Gabe'll back us up."

"I am sticking with no more secrets," Gabe replied, holding up his hands. "Look at me, being the good person."

"I'll buy you a drink," I offered.

"Are you sick with a cold or the stomach bug?" Gabe immediately asked, pulling out an imaginary pen and paper to take notes. "I gotta make sure I tell your boss the right thing."

All four of us dissolved into laughter, with Bastian holding his sides. It felt good to laugh after the past couple of days. Bastian pretended to punch Leo's broken arm. Leo made a show of wincing and then threatening to push him out window. Gabe mimed opening the window. They looked like twelve-year-old boys having a good time. It was hard to believe they were billionaires.

But these were my friends. I looked around the room, at the bright smiles and light-hearted camaraderie. This was my family. I loved two of these men like brothers and the third was my soul-mate. I couldn't be happier if I tried.

Together, we headed to the elevator. Gabe made fart jokes as we rode down that made me wonder how he ever got girls to go home with him.

Outside, the Florida sun was bright and hot. The air shimmered with heat and humidity and just breathing felt like I was being cooked alive. I missed my Caribbean ocean breezes keeping the heat to a tolerable level.

"You guys go on ahead," Leo said, catching my hand. "We'll catch up in just a minute."

Bastian narrowed his eyes. "Be good. She's still my sister and I'll still kick your ass."

"Oh, give the lovebirds a minute. You don't want to see them making out." Gabe made a gagging motion. "We'll meet you there."

Leo pulled on my hand, leading me around the corner of the building to a small nature area where employees could eat their lunches. A small man-made waterfall was the centerpiece with a little brook that meandered around the lunch area.

"I want to thank you, Charlotte," Leo said, pulling me to him. "You saved me."

I looked up into his blue eyes, seeing only love and a future of happiness within them. "I love you, Leo. You should know that by now."

He grinned and my heart pounded in my chest. Even after all that had happened, his smile still made me weak in the knees.

"I am the luckiest man in the world," he whispered, leaning down to press his lips to mine. Right before they touched, he breathed, "I love you."

And then he kissed me.

I kissed him back, the sound of the waterfall drowning out everything but him.

EPILOGUE

I never thought this day would come.

I look down at my white dress and giggle. It feels so surreal. I have to be dreaming, and this has to be the best dream of my life.

I'm going to marry Leo Westbrook.

I've dreamed of this day since I was thirteen years old, and now, finally, it's coming true.

"You ready, Char?" Chloe, my childhood best friend asks. She's grinning at me, looking gorgeous as usual. The same dark hair she shares with her brother is curled into perfect waves. "Everyone's waiting."

I take one last look in the mirror and then I nod.

I was born ready.

Just outside the door, Bastian is waiting. He's leaning against the wall, pretending to be calm and collected, but I know better. He's nervous. The tick in his jaw and the way the little scar above his eye is pulsing show me that he's nervous.

He smiles and his face softens as he sees me. "Wow," he whispers. "You look so beautiful."

I grin. "You don't look so bad yourself," I tell him. He stands up a little straighter and puffs out his chest.

"Eh, I thought I should dress for the occasion," he teases. He looks handsome in his dark gray suit with a small white lily in his lapel. He holds out his hand for mine. "Ready?"

I nod. "Are you?"

Instead of starting to walk, he pulls me into a hug, his big arms encircling me and holding me close. For a moment, I am not a grown woman. I am a small girl of five years old and he is my older brother, protecting me from the world.

"I love you. You are my sister," he whispers, his voice gruff.

I can't cry. Not yet. Crying is for when it's over.

"I've been ready for ten years," I remind him. Bastian laughs, releasing me from his hug.

He offers me his arm and I hold onto him as we walk to the ceremony.

Leo and I chose this place. It is just a mile away from the school campus where we first met, with a beautiful walkway winding through the trees. There is a small waterfall off to the side, the sound of water relaxing as it mixes with the music. I can see the backs of the chairs, all lined up and white against the greenery. But I can't see him yet.

In front of me, Ava, Chloe, and Emma walk to the music. They turn and walk down the aisle, disappearing one by one from my sight.

"You sure you want to do this?" Bastian asks as Ava, my maid of honor starts her walk. "I mean, it is Leo you're marrying."

I laugh. "Yes, I'm sure."

"Okay." Bastian shrugs. "Just giving you one last chance here." He smiles at me, and I know that he approves of my choice of husband. I'd actually be worried if he didn't tease me.

Bastian takes a deep breath as the music changes. Together we step out and into the aisle.

My friends are lined up on my left, but I barely notice them. I barely notice Gabe or Jack. The only person I see is Leo.

His face shifts from nervous to that of love. He grins at me as our eyes meet from across the room. Suddenly, none of it matters. The dress, the flowers, the location- none of it. I would marry that man wearing nothing but a paper-bag and carrying dandelions. As long as I got to marry him, I wouldn't care.

I float more than walk down the aisle, my eyes only for Leo. The closer I get, the brighter he smiles. I'm lost in his eyes as I step up to the alter.

"Who gives this woman to this man?" the pastor asks.

"I do," Bastian announces. His voice shakes with emotion. He kisses my cheek, tears in his eyes as he gives his little sister to the man of her dreams. He passes my hand to Leo's, my brother's hands strong and sure over mine. "Take care of her."

"I will," Leo promises, his eyes solemn.

Bastian lets me go and I step to stand next to Leo. He takes my hands in his. We're both shaking, but Leo's hands are strong and sure around mine.

"Dearly beloved, we are gathered here today to join this man and this woman in holy matrimony," the pastor begins, his voice rich and booming. "This is not entered into unadvisedly or lightly, but reverently and soberly. Into this estate, these to persons present come now to be joined. If any one can show just cause why they may not be lawfully joined together, let them speak now or forever hold their peace."

I hold my breath. It would be just like Gabe or Bastian to say something now or have hired someone to play a prank. No one says anything and the pastor nods, ready to continue with the ceremony.

Leo lets out a nervous laugh, apparently thinking the same thing I am.

"Leo, repeat after me..." the pastor waits until he has Leo's full

attention. "With this ring, I, Leo Westbrook take thee, Charlotte Page..."

"With this ring, I, Leo Westbrook, take thee, Charlotte Page..." The man of my dreams smiles as he begins his promise.

"... to be my wedded wife, to have and hold from this day forward, for better or worse, for richer for poorer, in sickness and in health, to love, honor, and cherish, 'til death do us part."

Leo repeats the words without hesitation. I love the way his voice flows, rising and falling with the words. I love the way he promises me to be mine forever. I fall a little bit more in love with him with every word.

"...'til death do us part," Leo finishes.

"Groomsman, the ring?" The pastor turns to Gabe.

"Um..." Gabe pats his pockets, his eyes going wide as he doesn't find anything.

I decide I might have to kill him, which is unfortunate because bloodstains will be difficult to get out of this dress.

"Gabe?" Leo's voice is low and full of warning. "Where is the ring?"

"Right here," Gabe replies with a grin, producing a small box from his jacket pocket. He winks at both of us, and I'm still considering killing him.

Chloe throws her bouquet at him. "Knock it off, Gabe."

They always did have the cutest sibling rivalry.

Leo takes the small box and takes out a ring. His hands are steady as he takes his grandmother's ring out and slides it along my finger. I love how it fits on my hand, like it was always meant to be there.

Leo grins and starts to lean forward, ready to kiss me.

"Hold on," the pastor says, putting his hand on Leo's shoulder and stopping him from kissing me. "Only one kiss per customer."

The audience laughs and Leo blushes.

"I just don't want to wait," he tells the pastor. "I want to kiss her always."

"Well, let her do her part and you can get to the kissing," the pastor tells him with a smile. "Now, Charlotte, repeat after me."

I say the words, my heart singing them out. "I, Charlotte Page, take thee, Leo Westbrook, to be my wedded husband, to have and hold from this day forward, for better or worse, for richer for poorer, in sickness and in health, to love, honor, and cherish, 'til death do us part."

Leo's ring is a solid gold band. I slide it along his left ring finger, biting my lip with concentration. It fits perfectly, as suited to him as mine is to me.

"Now, you may kiss the bride," the minister tells Leo with a chuckle.

"Good," Leo replies. "I've been waiting all day to do this."

He takes me into his arms, dipping me backwards and giving me a thorough and elaborate wedding kiss.

The crowd of our friends goes wild. Camera flashes fill the air, making it hard to see anything but sparkling lights. It's all right, because all I can see is Leo anyway. He's all I want to see.

And now he's all mine.

Slowly, he lets me back up, grinning wildly. "I love you, Charlotte," he whispers so that only I can hear him.

Behind him, the waterfall dances down the rocks, filling the small pond just like Leo fills my heart.

"I love you," I whisper back, grinning so hard my face hurts.

This is everything I could ever want: Leo and waterfall kisses.

Escape With Me: A Midlife Love Story

"I gave it all up to be happy. I'd give it all up again for you."

They say life begins after 40, but Cassie ain't feelin' it. Divorced and feeling trapped by her job, she wants to let loose for her friend's tropical beach wedding. She decides to let her hair down and get a little unpredictable. That's when she meets a handsome bartender, Wyatt.

Despite a few grey hairs, Wyatt's the liveliest man that Cassie has ever met. She knows that there's got to be more to his life story than just being a bartender, but this is just supposed to be a vacation fling. And after sunny days spent breaking all the rules on the beach together, Cassie realizes that nobody has ever listened to her the way that Wyatt does.

His carefree life is enviable, his kisses are intoxicating, and she can almost imagine a life with him. But all vacations come to an end. And when Cassie invites him to visit her hometown, Wyatt reveals that he can never go back. Not to her town. Not to America. Not to civilization.

Cassie leaves, confused and heartbroken, wondering just who she got herself involved with. Suddenly, her predictable life gets turned upside down when she sees her picture splashed across the Internet. And when the tabloids come looking for the mature woman who found the lost billionaire, she has no idea what to do…

…until he comes back.

Escape With Me: A Midlife Love Story

ABOUT THE AUTHOR

New York Times and USA Today Bestseller Krista Lakes is a thirtysomething who recently rediscovered her passion for writing. She is living happily ever after with her Prince Charming. Her first kid just started preschool and she is happy to welcome her second child into her life, continuing her "Happily Ever After"!

Thank you for supporting an indie author. Anything you can do, whether it be writing a review, or even simply telling a fellow reader that you enjoyed this, helps me out immensely. Thanks!

Krista would love to hear from you! Please contact her at Krista.Lakes@gmail.com or friend her on Facebook!

Further reading:

Bad Boys and Babies
>   Family Doctor's Baby
>   The Billionaire's Baby Arrangement
>   Crime Boss Baby

Kinds of Love
>   A Forever Kind of Love
>   A Wonderful Kind of Love
>   An Endless Kind of Love

Billionaires and Brides

Yours Completely: A Cinderella Love Story
Yours Truly: A Cinderella Love Story
Yours Royally: A Cinderella Love Story

The "Kisses" series

Saltwater Kisses: A Billionaire Love Story
Kisses From Jack: The Other Side of Saltwater Kisses
Rainwater Kisses: A Billionaire Love Story
Champagne Kisses: A Timeless Love Story
Freshwater Kisses: A Billionaire Love Story
Sandcastle Kisses: A Billionaire Love Story
Hurricane Kisses: A Billionaire Love Story
Barefoot Kisses: A Billionaire Love Story
Sunrise Kisses: A Billionaire Love Story
Waterfall Kisses: A Billionaire Love Story
Island Kisses: A Billionaire Love Story

Other Novels

I Choose You: A Secret Billionaire Romance
His Every Desire: A Billionaire Seduction
Wolf Six's Salvation: A Shifter Love Story
Burned: A New Adult Love Story
Walking on Sunshine: A Sweet Summer Romance
An American Cinderella: A Royal Love Story
Mr. Darcy's Kiss: A Contemporary Pride and Prejudice